D0839544

The Silent Victims

ALSO BY CAROLE O'NEILL

The Porch Sitters
Taylor's Truth
Shameful Truth
Hidden Truth

Anthology:
Goin' Coastal

Non-fiction:
Women in Media Careers

The Silent Victims

A Cozy Mystery

Carole O'Neill

This book is a work of fiction. Except for the brave souls who allowed me to use their real names, other names, characters, places, and incidents either are products of the author's imagination or are used fictitiously.

Copyright © 2022 by Carole O'Neill

All rights reserved

No portion of this book may be reproduced, stored in a retrieval system, or transmitted in any form or any means, electronic or mechanical, including photocopying without the prior written permission of the publisher – except by a reviewer who may quote brief passages in a review to be printed in a magazine or newspaper.

Front Cover Image: Photo by Rich Legg from istockphotos
Back Cover Image: Photo170771491/Shopping Mall
@Calvin L. Leake/Dreamtime

Published and distributed by:

COT Publishing
P.O. Box 3379
Myrtle Beach, South Carolina 29578

First printing December 2022
Printed in the United States of America

For Jim

After the first death there is no other.

~DYLAN THOMAS

Chapter One

It was darker than usual this morning as they skirted around corners in an attempt to keep up with the Millers. The jewelry kiosk was in sight. A landmark everyone used as proof they were almost at the end of their route. Could be the heavy fog blocking the forecasted white clouds from brightening the skylights along the main aisle inside the Seafarers Mall. The fog along the beach and downtown areas of Myrtle Beach had been difficult to manipulate. Drivers had trouble seeing the roads as soon as the fog rolled in by late afternoon. Most mornings it was close to noon before the fog rolled back out. The post-pandemic masks, still worn indoors by those with medical conditions, didn't make breathing any easier as they tried to match the pace they walked before the arrival of Covid. Deep breaths were hard to come by. Soon they would walk without facemasks.

"I need to rest in that rocking chair up ahead," said Mike Rodgers. His asthma was worse this fall. He kept telling his wife, Annette, he was suffering from pine pollen.

She wasn't convinced.

"If I stop now," she said, "I'll never complete today's goal. Take your time. I'll meet you at the food court."

As soon as he was seated, he pulled off his mask and inhaled as much air as his lungs would accept. He wondered how long it would be before he became dependent on oxygen. Maybe he would have to slow down his pace. Or stop mall walking altogether.

Mike heard the noise before he saw the keys hanging from the waist of the youngest member of the daily walkers. Jake carried more than two dozen danglers on a ring that attached to one of the loops on his pant waist. If he walked with just a slight limp, he could create a beat they could follow as they made their way to the goal line. Mike waited until the last of the walkers had passed and then joined the line. Theirs was a tight knit group, numbering fourteen. Usually travelling in a pack. They called themselves the eight-thirties. By nine o'clock the seniors from the trailer park would arrive and take over the main aisle. By then, Mike's group was usually seated around tables in the food court, enjoying coffee and bagels. Except, of course, for the double-loopers. Four women from the eight-thirties were working on a fitness program that required more steps.

The Millers had already arrived at the Starbucks' kiosk. First as usual. Mary decided to use the mall restroom while John ordered their decafs. As she rounded the corner leading down the hallway to the room marked "Ladies," she saw the foot. Her scream brought nearly a dozen of the walkers into the hallway. The shoeless man was not moving. One of the eight-thirties was a nurse. They called her cell and asked her to come quickly. When she arrived she checked his response and started CPR. Nothing. Jake made the 911 call. He was familiar with the procedure because his overnight security shift at the hospital often required a police visit. Especially in the emergency room. He knew not to allow anyone to touch a thing near the man on the floor. By now, the crowded hallway needed to be cleared. He swung into action with familiarity, making sure everyone knew not to leave the area. Most of the eight-thirties were in the coffee line as the sirens got closer. Minutes later, several officers and EMT's entered the doors closest to the food court.

After the police arrived, and the crime scene crew began their routine, each of the walkers was interviewed for the record. Detective Collins knew when the shops at the mall opened for business the shoppers would fill the aisles and clues could be missed. He assumed they would need more time and called for back-up to block each of the mall entrances until they could finish their initial investigation. His men began walking the entire mall to see if any of the merchants had already entered their shop. There were four department stores and thirty-five merchants along the perimeter. The kiosks running down the middle of the aisles numbered twenty-four. A huge task for any police department to cover, let alone a crime scene unit devoted mostly to tourist problems along the boardwalk as well as thefts and the occasional gang shooting within the hotels along the beach.

This was the second body found at the mall in less than two months. Detective Collins was already under the gun to complete the previous investigation. So far, they had no suspects, and no motives. Basically, no leads. The Myrtle Beach Police Department's Crime Unit was working day and night for clues. Their reputation was on the line.

Crime scene tape roped off the hallway and orange cones were placed along a path in front of several fast-food counters across the room from Starbucks. Most of the eight-thirties sat at tables in front of the coffee kiosk watching the events unfold. Many drinking way more coffee than usual. Those who normally went to work after their walk had to notify their employers of the delay. Patience was not on display as they waited to be released. The only walker with any factual information was Mary. No one saw anything along the aisles before she discovered the body. It took nearly an hour for her to appear calm. She said each time she closed her eyes, she saw only the foot. His bare foot. She wondered if he slept there overnight. There was no identification on him according to the police. She assured them she had never seen the man before.

Detective Collins held a meeting of the officers who had walked the perimeter of the mall looking for anyone who might have opened their shop early. The only merchant in any of the shops was Brandy Sommers. Seaside Treasures was one of the smaller self-contained spaces along the side aisle leading to Dowds, the largest department store in the mall.

"She claims to have seen nothing since arriving at eight o'clock," Officer Stone informed his boss, looking through the pages in his notepad. He had worked in the CSI unit since Detective Collins took over three years ago.

"Does she always get here that early?" asked Collins, "seems unusual."

"There were at least a dozen boxes unpacked and stacked in a corner," said Stone walking over to show Collins a picture on his phone. "Says she needed to get this new merchandise on display before the store opened."

"Looks like a lot of broken glass to me," said Collins.

"If you look close chief, they all have shapes like letters of the alphabet." He tapped his phone and enlarged one of the pictures. "You can see this green glass is shaped like an S. She says they are finely cut by a jeweler in Bermuda. Costs a pretty penny, too."

"That all you got?"

"Yeah. Only owner here right now. She says she came in the north doors by Dowds. Never even drove by the south side of the mall. She started shaking when I asked about the body. I think I spooked her. Dialed her husband as I was leaving. Another body around here is not very comforting for these merchants."

"I don't need to hear that from you, Stone." Detective Collins walked toward the food court entrance as the EMT's were bringing in the stretcher.

"Getting a body bag?" he asked, turning to follow them toward the hallway. "Has the coroner finished?"

"Yeah. We're taking him to the morgue. Might be a homicide. There's a blood clot on the inside of his right hand. Some dried blood in his mouth. Could have been lying here several hours. He'll know more after he examines him back in his corner of the world."

Detective Collins froze in place when he heard the word homicide. "Er. So, you don't think this guy just had a heart attack? I didn't see any gun or knife wound? You talkin' poison of some kind?"

"Like he said, Chief, I'll know more after a thorough examination," said the Horry County Medical Examiner. He moved away from the body. "Go ahead, boys. Bag him." He finished packing his instruments in his bag. "I'll give you a call when I have a definitive cause, Detective." He went into the mall and walked out the food court doors.

Collins moved like he was walking on beach sand. Unsteady. His eyes stared beyond the crowd waiting to hear they could finally go home. He looked for Officer Stone.

"Get the squad together," he said when he caught up

with two of the newest members of his unit. He pointed to the eight-thirties sitting at the tables across the room. "Make sure you have everyone's contact information before you let them go. And have the guys meet me at the mall office. The manager has arrived, and we'll need a base location while we interview every store employee in this building. Looks like this guy might have been here last night."

The officers worked in pairs and by ten-thirty most of the morning employees had been asked about the barefoot man. Margie Kane couldn't wait for the police to leave her area. She ran the fragrance counter at Dowds. Making sure she had as many details as possible was her goal. Everyone went to her for the latest gossip in the mall. She had her sources at the other department stores as well as a few leakers working in the south side stores. It was hard to keep any secrets from Margie.

"So, Officer Stone did you say?" He never said. She read his nametag on his uniform. "Have you spoken to Daniel Logan yet?"

"Does he work here at Dowds?"

"Oh, no. He owns Kitchen Cutlery two doors down from Rack Room Shoes."

"Do you think he knows this man?"

"Well, I'm not sure about that, Officer. But he has been a person of interest in the death behind the Olive Shop a few weeks ago."

"Thank you, ma'am. We'll be sure to check him out." As the stores began opening their doors for the morning shoppers, questions about the police presence spread quickly.

By the time Ellen O'Connell opened the doors of her Olive Shop, she had decided there was no way she would go through another month of questioning and accusations. The police still hadn't confirmed the cause of death on the woman found five weeks ago behind her shop. That covered alleyway was a favorite haunt for the homeless population in the town, especially when it rained.

Ellen knew there would be at least two or three other merchants willing to pool their money so they could hire their own private investigator. She had met Beulah Jean Pickens at a Chamber of Commerce event. She found the Private Investigator's card and made the call.

Chapter Two

Beulah Jean waited for the sky to clear before taking Miss Shelby out for her morning walk. Too often she would take a chance, only to be drenched with the last batch of rain from a passing storm. The result would require a yeoman's work for the private investigator. There was nothing more challenging than drying her golden retriever's long mane.

They were crossing Farrow Parkway when her phone rang. The number was not one she recognized, so she pushed the forward option to send the call to her office voicemail. A stop at Peace, Love & Little Donuts took preference. She had developed an addiction to the sweet treats, especially the Salted Caramel Macchiatos. Could hardly go a day without one. Addicted. The fault was Jack Handy's. He introduced her to the habit last fall, one of the many for which she had grown accustomed. Like the long weekends they spent together at his place on the Isle of Palms. Even though he would prefer they spend every night together, any discussion of closing her private investigation office in Market Common was a non-starter.

She saw the flashing red light on her office phone when she entered and walked over to hang up Miss Shelby's leash. After choosing a flavored coffee from her Keurig, she sat down at her desk. The dog settled into her favorite spot underneath, half of her body resting on her master's foot. After a bite of her donut, Beulah Jean pushed the red button on the answering machine.

The high-pitched voice filled the room. "Detective Pickens, this is Ellen O'Connell. I'm the owner of the Olive Shop over here at the Seafarers Mall. I met you when you spoke at a Chamber meeting a couple months ago. We have a situation that requires a competent investigator. Someone like you. Please call me back. Er, okay. Thanks."

Beulah Jean noted how she didn't leave a number. That was never a good sign. She googled the Olive Shop and placed the call.

"Ms. O'Connell, this is Beulah Jean Pickens returning your call. What can I do for you?" She made it a practice to learn all the particulars before agreeing to work an investigation. Eighteen years with the Monks Corner Police Department taught her not everyone's emergency needed an experienced detective. Sometimes giving out a proper phone number for a different town office would solve the problem.

"Oh, yes, Ms. Pickens. A dead body was discovered here this morning. We are all beside ourselves."

"Was the body found in your shop?"

"Oh, goodness no. Somewhere near the restrooms. I'm not sure of the exact location, but last month a body was found in the alley behind my shop. Since then, the police have practically lived here. I can't go through another day under their suspicious eyes."

Beulah Jean remembered reading the report in the Sun News. "Have they solved that mystery, yet?"

"They haven't charged anyone with the crime, and according to everyone we talk to here, they don't seem to have any leads." Her voice softened as she spoke with someone in her shop. "I'm getting to that," she said with increasing volume. "A few of the shop owners have agreed to chip in and get our own investigator. We need our names cleared. I was telling everyone about the drug dealer you helped capture. They were all sold on retaining you before I finished the story. Our hope is that you'll have time to accept our request."

Beulah Jean was grateful for the networking process the Chamber afforded her through her membership. She didn't believe in traditional advertising. When she was a member of the police force, nothing like that was required. Her transition into the private sector had revealed some of her new constraints.

"I would be happy to meet with you to see if I can help. In the case of murder, the local police force would make the arrest. I could, however, look into clearing your names. Why don't I stop by this afternoon?"

When she arrived outside the mall, the number of roped-off areas required extra time to find a place to park her powder blue VW convertible bug. Once inside, she observed several officers walking throughout the building. Beulah Jean found the Olive Shop and saw a middle-aged woman dressed completely in black at the counter in the back of the store. Long gold olive leaf earrings hung from each ear.

She was bagging several bottles of balsamic vinegar and fig oil for a young couple wearing matching green shirts.

The black italic writing on the back of their shirts read; *Olive Me Loves Olive You.*

When the sale was complete, Beulah Jean asked, "Are you Ellen O'Connell?"

"Yes. I recognized you from the Chamber meeting. Thank you for coming Ms. Pickens. Let me make a quick call. A few of the other store owners want to be included when we meet."

Beulah Jean walked over to the shelves holding different varieties of olive oil and vinegar. The names on the bottles piqued her interest. Blood Orange and Meyer Lemon Olive Oil were listed as the most popular on the brochure handout. While Cranberry Pear White topped the list of Balsamic Vinegars. She decided to buy a selection to offer Jack the next time he came for dinner. She gathered her choices and brought them to the counter.

"I couldn't resist these," she said, handing them to Ellen along with her credit card.

"Let me give you my employee discount. My hope is you'll take our case and make it official." She rang up the sale and introduced the two shop owners who had walked up behind Beulah Jean.

"Ms. Pickens, this is Dan Logan, the owner of Kitchen Cutlery, and Brandy Sommers, the owner of Seaside Treasures. They couldn't wait to meet you."

They all shook hands and Ellen led them into her private office. She asked her salesclerk to take over.

"I'll be off the clock during this meeting," she told the teenage blonde in the short skirt and high-top sneakers. "Please make sure we aren't disturbed."

Ellen offered everyone coffee and soft drinks before she began reporting on the day's events.

"As soon as I drove into the parking lot this morning, I knew things were bad," she began. "I could see the police cars through the fog, and the ambulance at the food court entrance. A reminder of the nightmare I've been going through for the past five weeks."

"I got here before the police," said Brandy. "I had no idea they found another body. It was really quiet at my end of the mall. Didn't even notice the mall walkers this morning."

"I never see the mall walkers," said Dan.

"That's because they're gone by the time we open at 11:00 a.m.," offered Ellen.

Beulah Jean made a note to check out these early morning visitors at the mall.

"Before we go any further, what can you tell me about the person they found last month?"

Ellen pulled a pad from the top drawer of a file cabinet, then handed it to Beulah Jean.

"These are the notes I've taken each time the police have questioned me. They found a woman's body behind my shop five weeks ago. There's a covered alleyway out back running the length of four stores. We've become aware of how attractive the space is to the homeless population. She has never been identified. I'm not convinced she lived outdoors. No one has filed a missing person's report. The mall management just wants the entire situation to end. Now this."

Beulah Jean flipped through the pad, stopping at one page.

"This note refers to questions about your involvement. Did you find the body?"

"Yes. I was taking my garbage out to the dumpster when I saw her lying on the ground," said Ellen.

"I thought she had slept there overnight."

"You say she still hasn't been identified?"

"No. They keep coming here to see if I'll admit to doing something to her. They have never called it a homicide because they have no proof. I think her death is listed as one from natural causes."

Dan pulled out his cell phone and showed Beulah Jean the police picture of the dead woman.

"I brought this over to the park where several homeless people spend their days. No one recognized her. I'm not convinced they weren't protecting someone. Look at how she was dressed. To me, the clothing says everything."

"Those bell-bottom pants are coming back in style," said Beulah Jean. "I will admit the shredded hem looks like they were dragged through the dirt. Did she have shoes hidden under that fabric?"

"There were no shoes on her or anywhere in the area that I could see," said Ellen.

"This guy they found this morning was also barefoot," said Dan. "The police told me when they questioned me."

"Yeah. They've posted information at each entrance asking the public for their help, hoping someone can identify him," said Brandy.

"When they questioned me today," said Ellen, I felt like I was living the nightmare all over again. No clues, no leads, no closure. Please, Ms. Pickens, we need your help. Will you take our case?"

Beulah Jean pulled a contract out of her tote bag. "You'll each need to read this over carefully. If you agree to the terms, I can start first thing in the morning. I'll need to stop at the Myrtle Beach Police Station this afternoon. Their cooperation will be important. Sometimes another pair of trained eyes is welcome. Other times, there's resentment. I did work with them on my last case over at Market Common. They're aware of my credentials and experience. I don't believe there will be a problem. Just want to check in."

Dan pulled a pen out of his shirt pocket, signed the contract, and passed it to Brandy. "I'm on board. Whatever you need. My shop is four doors down on the right."

"I'm also in," said Brandy. She signed the contract and gave it to Ellen.

Ellen added her signature. "I already feel a weight has been lifted from my shoulders," she said. "Maybe it's my Catholic upbringing, but I feel like I have a guardian angel working to clear my name."

"I've never been called an angel, but I will do my best to solve this mystery."

Chapter Three

On the way back to her office, Beulah Jean stopped by the Myrtle Beach Police Station. She was told Detective Collins was handling the Mall cases. After locating his office, she introduced herself to his secretary and asked to meet with him.

"Your reputation precedes you, Ms. Pickens." Detective Collins stood at his desk and offered his hand to shake. "Are you looking to fill the opening in our Investigative Division? You'd have my support."

"Thanks Detective Collins," she said, shaking his hand, "but I'm quite happy where I am. I was wondering if you could give me an update on those open cases at the mall. A few of the shop owners are hoping I can clear their names."

"Please, call me Doug. After your lead on the drug takedown, I'm surprised you need my help at all."

He smiled and gestured for her to sit down. "The truth is we have no leads on either case. Let me pull up the Jane

Doe file from last month."

Beulah Jean sat in the chair across from his desk and took out her notebook.

"We assume she had no family in the area," said Collins. "No one called in a missing person's report. Officers Stone and Wexler followed the initial investigation until we placed everything in the open unsolved files. There's something strange about that case if you ask me. It appeared as though the woman was dead for some time before she was discovered by one of the shop owners. However, no one saw her there the night before. Our latest theory is that someone placed her in that location after the mall was closed up tight. No fingerprints were left. Almost like she flew to that spot and dropped like a feather seeking flat land."

"What about security lights in the area?" asked Beulah Jean.

"We discovered none of the lights around the outside of the mall were working properly," said Collins. "Not sure if they were intentionally broken so there would be no way to see clearly, or if they just stopped working on their own?

"I've spoken to the woman who found the body," said Beulah Jean. "She's one of the owners who hired me. Says you guys had her jumping through hoops for days. She's still dealing with remnants of the ordeal. Did you think she was responsible for something besides the discovery?"

"You understand how that goes, Ms. Pickens. We hang on to what seems likely until there's nothing left to hold. She found the body. Nothing else came close."

"What was the official cause of death?" asked Beulah Jean.

"Undetermined."

"So, Ms. O'Connell is no longer a suspect?"

"She'll always remain a 'person of interest,' along with two or three other shop owners, until we officially close the case."

She was beginning to understand why they felt it necessary to hire their own investigator.

"Hell, I'd hire you myself," said Collins "if I thought that's all it would take to put a period on the end of that mystery."

"So, you have no problem with my digging into Jane Doe's death. What about the latest body? The man near the restroom. Are there any similarities?"

"Stone and Wexler have picked up that case, as well.

Might be connected. Not sure, yet. They are heavy into the fact gathering phase. You'll see them over at the mall. I'll let them know it's okay to share their findings with you. I'm sure I don't have to ask the same favor of you"

"Thanks for your time, sir. I appreciate your help and you know I'll do right by you".

Beulah Jean hoped she could get more information from the officers handling the case. There wasn't a lot to go on. Looked like she would have to begin from scratch. In the morning she'd start asking questions of those mall walkers the owners mentioned.

The alarm woke her earlier than normal. She realized if she wanted to question the mall walkers, she'd have to get there before having her first cup of coffee. After letting Miss Shelby out in the yard to take care of her necessities, she put on her jogging clothes. By 8:15a.m. she had settled her dog in her upstairs living quarters and left for the mall. She wanted to be set up when the walkers completed their routine and were enjoying their coffee.

About ten cars were parked near the food court entrance when she arrived. An older couple walked towards the door together, holding hands. The woman seemed to be steadying the man as he leaned left. She wondered if she and Jack would ever get to that stage in their relationship. When they found the time to walk together now, they either circled the lake at Market Common or avoided turtle nests in the sand on the Isle of Palms. She wasn't ready to look beyond their routine.

After entering the building, she found a table across the aisle from the Starbucks' kiosk. The aroma of coffee beans tested her patience as she waited for the place to open. Through the zippered window, a small man could be seen taking paper cups from a box and placing them on the counter behind the display case filled with breakfast pastries. Even from that distance, she made the decision to purchase one of the blueberry scones.

Her body tensed as she stood when she saw the dog coming toward her at full speed. An officer pulled on the leash and gave the animal a command.

Beulah Jean found herself breathing heavy. Not something she expected.

"Sorry ma'am, I didn't realize anyone would be here at this hour." He shortened the leash and walked over next to

Beulah Jean. "I usually keep him closer. Are you okay?" The dog sat in a frozen position next to the Officer's right leg.

"Yes, I'm fine. I'm a private investigator waiting to interview some of the walkers here this morning." She shook his hand, and said with confidence, "B.J. Pickens."

"Officer Stone never told me you'd be here. Is he expecting you?"

"No, I don't think so, but I met with Detective Collins yesterday. He was going to inform Officers Stone and Wexler about my involvement."

"They're both meeting with him as we speak. I'm sure they'll update me when they arrive. I was asked to take Roscoe through the building before the stores opened. Yesterday we spent most of our time in and around the restrooms. I did one run through the mall before the cleaning crew came in last night. Just making sure I didn't overlook any nooks or crannies."

"Did you discover anything of note?"

"My written report should be available later today. Until I speak with Officer Stone, I'd rather leave it at that."

She could tell this man was going by the book.

—

"No, problem. Don't let me keep you. I see the coffee kiosk has opened. I'll get my breakfast before the walkers reach the end of their route."

She had taken the last bite of her scone when the woman entered the food court, only a few steps ahead of a man in a matching sweatshirt. Beulah Jean assumed they were a couple. She watched them choose a table before the woman went over to Starbucks and came back with coffees and a bag of bagels. Over the next ten minutes nearly a dozen walkers filled the tables in the food court. Each one eventually enjoying a purchase from the only vendor open in the area.

Beulah Jean approached the couple with the matching sweatshirts. She didn't want them to leave before she had a chance to ask a few questions.

"Excuse me, I'm Private Investigator, Beulah Jean Pickens," she said handing them her cards. "I was wondering if I could ask you a few questions about the man found yesterday near the restroom?"

"Mary was the woman who found him," said the man

pointing to his wife. "We're the Millers. I'm John. She screamed so loud I thought she was being killed. Nearly caused me to have a heart attack."

"I told the police everything I knew," said Mary crossing her arms over her chest, putting an end to her cooperation.

"Yes. I understand Detective Collins was quite thorough. However, even though the crime scene crew is sharing their information, I've been hired by a few of the shop owners, because of the death of the woman last month. They feel a new set of eyes will help clear their names."

Mary uncrossed her arms and spoke softer. "That was a shame. We never saw that dead body, thank God. They still haven't found the murderer."

"You think she was murdered?"

"Well," said John, "the Sun News called it murder. Never retracted that statement." He yelled over to a table in the corner. "Hey, Mike, what's the latest on that woman's murder last month? Have you heard anything that would lead you to believe there might be a connection between her death and the man Mary found yesterday?"

The man she saw leaning on the woman outside the mall

got up from his table and joined them. He walked with a slight limp and breathed heavily.

"Mike knows everyone over at the paper. He gets the scoop for us on all our issues. Especially the ones that affect our lives, like the new redistricting recommendations."

Beulah Jean had read all about the redistricting issues. She wasn't sure how she felt about what would happen in Market Common. Many Myrtle Beach homeowners were threatening protests. These retirees definitely had a preference.

When Mike got to their table, he pulled out his rescue inhaler and took two puffs. John introduced him to Beulah Jean.

"Investigator Pickens is asking about the two dead bodies," he told Mike. "She wondered if there were any similarities."

Mike sat down. He was definitely out of breath. "You mean, besides being dead." He motioned for his wife to join them. "There is the question of how they died. And, of course, why here at the mall? I mean, the guy was barefoot. We have sixty miles of beach nearby. Why inside here?

Beulah Jean felt the discussion going in the wrong direction. She addressed Mike. "Did you actually see either body?"

"Hell, no," said Mike. "My wife, Annette, ran to support Mary yesterday, right after she heard her scream." He put his arm around the woman Beulah Jean assumed was his wife.

"Annette, can you tell me anything about the man you saw in the restroom yesterday morning?"

"My first instinct was to see if he was dead or just sleeping off a bad night on alcohol or drugs. I called Pat right away." She looked straight in Beulah Jean's eyes. "Pat Coloe. She's a nurse."

"Is she here this morning?" asked Beulah Jean.

"She's one of our double-loopers. They're on their second trip around. She should be here in another twenty minutes or so."

"Can you describe what the man looked like?"

"I've actually been forcing myself not to think about him at all. I see pieces of him when I concentrate. Like his bare feet. The trickle of blood near his hand," she stopped.

"I think he was close to forty, maybe. He had a well-defined five o'clock shadow. Couldn't tell you the color of his eyes. They were closed. He was wearing a wedding ring. My guess is someone should be filing a missing person's report soon."

"You said you saw blood?"

"Did you notice that drop of blood on the floor under his hand, Annette?" asked Mary getting up and walking closer to her friend.

"Yeah, I think there was something in that hand, although it was closed tight," said Annette. "I don't know if Pat tried to open it to see if there was a cut on his palm she could treat."

"Do you think any of the other walkers saw him up close before the police arrived?" asked Beulah Jean.

"Jake might have had a better look. He pretty much took over blocking off the area. He's in security at the hospital. He's the guy walking into Starbucks with all the keys hanging from his belt. He could have noticed something I didn't see. I was really more concerned about Mary. She was as white as my printer paper. Thought she might faint."

"Sounds like you watch out for one another," said Beulah Jean.

"There isn't one of the eight-thirties I wouldn't trust

with my life," said Annette.

"I'm looking forward to meeting more members of your group," said Beulah Jean. She saw the man with the keys leaving Starbucks and walking toward their table. The number of people in the area seemed to grow by the minute. She knew then it was going to be a long day.

Chapter Four

Four more mall walkers arrived at the food court. Beulah Jean assumed they were the ones referred to as the 'double loopers.' She was amused, and frankly a little jealous, at the dedication they brought to the task. She'd always heard about the people who went to the mall each morning to get their exercise. The scene before her eyes destroyed her assumption that a group of seniors strolled by the stores for something to do in their retirement. These people were serious.

"I hear you're looking into the case of the body found near the restroom yesterday morning," said the man with all the keys as he approached Beulah Jean.

"Yes, I was told you took over crowd control before the police arrived."

"I'm not sure how much control I had over that group, But I was trying not to disturb the crime scene. My name is Jake."

"I'm Investigator Pickens," she said handing him one of

her cards.

"So, you felt confident a crime had been committed."

"I wasn't sure. Just responded to Pat's request that I call for the EMT's. She wasn't able to get a pulse. She even tried to resuscitate him without success."

"Is she here this morning? I'd like to ask her a few questions."

He waved to a petite woman leaving the Starbucks' kiosk. "Pat," he yelled louder than necessary, "can you come here a minute?"

"This is Pat Coloe," Jake said when she got close enough to rest his arm on her shoulder. "Investigator Pickens here is hoping you'll answer her questions."

The woman with the short blonde hair placed her cup of hot water on the table and worked the tea bag until she was satisfied with the color, then looked up at Beulah Jean.

"I told the police pretty much everything I know," said Pat.

"I will be reviewing all the statements from yesterday," said Beulah Jean letting this woman know she had some authority. "Jake mentioned that you tried to revive the man. Does that mean you detected a pulse when you arrived? Was the body still warm? What about the blood?"

"When I got to the scene, I noticed blood on the floor near his hand. But the blood was the least of my worries. He was unresponsive and was not breathing. I told Jake to call 911 and I started CPR."

"When I spoke with Detective Collins at the Myrtle Beach Police Department," said Beulah Jean, "he informed me of their quick response because of the body found last month. They were monitoring the dispatch assignments in the area."

"Yes. They actually arrived at the same time as the EMTs."

"Did the EMTs continue with the CPR process?"

"They took over CPR and used their defibrillator with no response from the man. They stopped after speaking with an ER Doctor. It became obvious the man was dead. They called the coroner. I left before the coroner arrived."

"Did the police ask you to go over to the station so they could eliminate your fingerprints?"

"That wasn't necessary. My prints have been in the national database since I took my first job at a hospital in New York."

"Did your nursing experience offer any expertise about the man's cause of death?"

"For the last twenty years of my career I worked as a school nurse. Not a lot of practice with dead bodies," she said with sarcasm.

Beulah Jean realized she had moved to an uncomfortable place. She didn't want to appear harsh. "Thanks Pat. Would you be willing to give me your contact information in case I think of something after I read the detailed notes from the police?" She handed Pat her opened notebook and a pen.

"Of course," said Pat. She wrote down her phone number and smiled when she looked at the investigator. "I was glad to be able to help yesterday. I kinda miss the days when my training was needed."

Beulah Jean noticed how the crowd began to thin. She wanted to make sure anyone who saw anything yesterday was willing to be questioned. She asked Jake to pass the word that she was interested in their information.

Over the next hour, four or five other walkers stopped by her table and offered details of their experience. This was definitely a strange case. No identification, no one looking for a missing person and the coroner hadn't listed the cause of death.

Driving back to Market Common, Beulah Jean remembered how the merchants who hired her questioned the dead man's bare feet. Yet the walkers made very little reference to that fact.

Miss Shelby bounded down the stairs and greeted her with her usual rub on each of Beulah Jean's legs. She patted the golden retriever and opened the back door to let her out in the yard. It was a long time for the old girl to wait. Now that she was close to fourteen, some of her needs became more urgent. They were both feeling quite comfortable in their townhouse in Market Common. Next month it would be a year since their move from Moncks Corner. So much had happened over the last twelve months. Not the least of which was meeting Jack. If her cousin, Beatrice, hadn't convinced her neighbors to hire Beulah Jean to find the thief breaking into houses on the Isle of Palms, she might not have met their local detective. Even though she swore she would never get involved again with anyone in law enforcement, he has made his way into her heart.

She sat down at her desk and clicked on the file sent from Detective Collins. Something about the report drew her attention. One of the walkers she spoke with this morning mentioned the dead man was wearing a wedding band. She picked up the phone and dialed.

The male voice answered, "Investigative Division, Collins speaking."

"Doug, this is Beulah Jean, thanks for the report you sent. I'm wondering if the coroner mentioned removing John Doe's ring. Thought maybe there was a woman's name engraved inside. Also, did you ever find shoes for the woman who was found behind the Olive Shop?"

"Wow. Agent Sullivan wasn't kidding when he said you were an exceptional investigator."

"I didn't realize you were still working with Agent Sullivan."

"I'm not. After you stopped by the precinct yesterday, I gave him a call. He praised your work on the take down of that drug dealer in Market Common. Said if you hadn't identified the man, he would still be on the case."

"That was very thoughtful of him," said Beulah Jean.

"Sullivan is not a thoughtful man, he's tough and plays by the rules. He doesn't hand out compliments. There's no question he thinks of you as a worthy colleague. Told me I was lucky to have your input on this case."

"Well, I hope I can live up to those words. I must admit, this case is challenging. Still no missing person's report?"

"No. But you've piqued my interest in that ring. Let me call the coroner and I'll get back to you. And, by the way, we never found any shoes for Jane Doe."

The front door opened, and Miss Shelby stepped on her foot trying to get out from under her desk to greet the visitor. Beulah Jean smiled when she saw who was walking into her office.

"Thanks, Doug. Let's hope the coroner breaks our log jam. Anxious to hear what he has to say."

She felt the kiss on the back of her neck as she hung up the phone.

"Hello, Gorgeous," said Jack backing up to give her room to stand.

"Hey, I wasn't expecting you for hours. How'd you get away so early?" She stood and gave him a proper welcoming kiss.

"I had to drop some papers off at SLED's Georgetown office. I wanted to talk to the sheriff before he left for the day. Besides any excuse to spend more time with the love of my life." He took her face in his hands and kissed her on the nose.

"I was planning a special dinner," said Beulah Jean. "Even planned to use this exceptional olive oil I bought from my new client, but I haven't started a thing."

"What was the name of that Italian restaurant your neighbor two doors down recommended?" asked Jack. "You know, the redhead who has the miniature poodle. The dog that sits in the expensive pocketbooks for sale."

"You mean Shannon. I think she called the place Maggie Ds."

"How 'bout you save that special dinner for tomorrow night and let me take you out for Italian."

"Sounds good to me, but it's a little early for dinner."

"My sentiments exactly," he said kissing her hand and then moving his lips up her arm.

She locked the door and put up the 'closed' sign.

They walked upstairs trying to dodge Miss Shelby as she headed for the bedroom.

Chapter Five

Maggi Ds was busy, but still felt intimate. Frank Sinatra's velvety voice was just loud enough to give you the feeling of being entertained while you dined. Jack and Beulah Jean took seats at the bar.

"What can I get you to drink?" asked the forty-something female bartender. She wore her black hair up on top of her head with a few wisps framing her face. She looked out into the restaurant to a table on the main floor. Beulah Jean assumed the bartender was handling more than the customers sitting at the bar. Her body language proved she was capable of double duty.

"I'll have a Yuengling draft," said Jack, "and the lady will have a Pino Grigio."

While she was pouring the beer, the short man sitting at the end of the bar yelled into the kitchen, "Robin, get the door and put them at table eleven." He used a magic marker and put an X over a square on the tiny white board he kept on the counter in front of his bar stool. They soon learned he was the owner, and his name was John. The hair on his head wasn't much longer than the peach fuzz on the chin of the young man cleaning tables. A moment later John asked the bartender, "Cynthia, can you take this order?" as he limped over to hand the bartender the phone before pouring the final inch of Jack's beer. He placed the drink in front of Jack and asked Beulah Jean, "What kind of wine was that you ordered?" He obviously didn't miss a trick.

"Will you folks be eating at the bar tonight?" he asked when he delivered Beulah Jean's wine.

"I think we will," she said.

John put two place settings in front of them and said, "Cynthia will be with you shortly." They obviously operated as a team, with no question of who was really in charge.

"So, tell me about this new case you're working," said Jack. "A dead John Doe in the mall?"

"It appears that way. At least no identification has been found, yet. The merchants who hired me think there might be a connection to the woman found dead behind the Olive

Shop last month."

"And what does your gut tell you?"

"That I need a lot more information. The investigators on the force don't have enough to tie the cases together, and individually both bodies seem to be missing enough facts to close their case."

"Sounds challenging," said Jack. "Did you get a chance to look into last month's victim?"

"The coroner has already sent her body to the Medical University of South Carolina under the required South Carolina Code of Laws."

"So, you have thirty days before they move into the next phase?"

"Yes. I'm afraid it's become time sensitive if I'm going to try to tie the cases together."

"Any positive angles on your plate?"

"Well, there might be a lead if there's anything written on the inside of the dead man's wedding band. Detective Collins is checking that out."

"Pretty weak," said Jack. "Could be initials. Maybe a date. Not much to go on."

"I'm grasping at straws right now. Nothing promising,"

The bartender stood in front of them with her pad and pencil.

"Let me tell you about our specials," offered Cynthia. "We have our normal Friday night lasagna, and tonight we also have a chicken and sausage special with peppers and onions over pasta."

She excused herself to make a marguerita for another waitress.

"Sorry folks," she said walking back to them. "The crowd hasn't slowed since lunch time. Lots of activity across the street, lately. They found someone dead yesterday."

"Have you heard who it was?" Jack asked giving Beulah Jean a wink.

"Nope. Just like last month," said Cynthia. "That poor woman was never identified. It's a little scary if you ask me. People are worried about going to the mall in the evening."

"Do you see many homeless people hanging out in the mall parking lot after dark?" asked Beulah Jean.

"Not really," said Cynthia. "Last winter during that cold spell a few homeless people were found enjoying the heated building overnight. That's when the mall owners decided to lock all the doors between midnight and six in the morning. They had security checking to make sure no one was locked inside. Some residents in the new luxury apartments behind us complained of a few homeless men hanging outside their front lobby. Otherwise, they stay pretty much down by the trailer parks."

Beulah Jean found the information helpful. The man must have been alive before six unless someone placed the dead body in the area where he was found before midnight the night before. She also made a mental note to check out the luxury apartments and the trailer parks.

"I'll have your lasagna special with a Caesar salad," said Beulah Jean.

"Make it two," added Jack.

"I'll be right back with your salads and some warm bread," said Cynthia.

The seats at the bar soon filled with customers who all appeared to be regulars. John would begin making their drinks before they even settled on their bar stools. "How are you two, tonight? He'd say placing their drinks and menus in front of them. Moments later, Cynthia would move in to announce the daily special.

Soon the owner and his bartender would begin sparring with one another issuing accusations of falling down on their duties. Beulah Jean found the entertainment as enjoyable as the Comedy Club out on Kings Highway.

"So, what can you tell me about the merchants who hired you?" asked Jack. "You said Detective Collins found them to be 'people of interest.'"

"Well, one of them, for sure. The woman who owns the Olive Shop. She found the first body in back of her store when she was emptying the trash. There's a sort of alley that runs the length of a couple of stores back there. I guess they felt she had more information than she was willing to share with them."

"Do you agree with that assessment?"

"I'm not sure. She was pretty forthcoming with me yesterday. I think she's told them everything she knows or can remember. The problem is there's nothing solid to go on with that case. One of the merchants said he took a picture of the woman over to the area where the homeless have lunch to see if anyone recognized her. I'm sure the Myrtle Beach Investigative Unit already covered that possibility, but I don't have the complete files they've compiled on her."

Cynthia brought them their main course and poured them a second round of drinks. After two bites Beulah Jean was hooked. "This is the best Lasagna I've had since leaving home. My mother's version might even drop to a close second."

She and Jack spent the next few minutes enjoying the flavor of John's mother's recipe. They decided this place would be a regular stop on their exploration of Myrtle Beach restaurants.

"What about the other merchants paying for your services?" asked Jack after cleaning his plate.

"What about them?"

"Do you think they have something to hide and are hoping you'll clear their names?"

"I don't know enough about either of them to confirm or deny their involvement. One owns a cutlery shop with expensive knives, the other owns Seaside Treasures. Sea glass is her specialty. I'm planning to visit both of them in their shops so I can get a look for myself. Each of them has been investigated because of the things they sell. I guess the detectives feel knives or glass could be used as weapons.

Although without reading the files, I'm not sure whether there were any wounds on either body.

"There must be something that has them following that trail," said Jack. "Do they have an official cause of death on this latest victim?"

"Not yet. But there was some mention of blood on the floor. So, I suppose sharp glass, or a knife could be the cause."

Cynthia began clearing their plates. "How about some dessert tonight, or maybe a cappuccino? We have homemade cheesecake, or a cannoli. Then there's our popular light offering of Limoncello Cake."

"I'll try a piece of your cheesecake and a cappuccino," said Jack.

"I'll settle for a cappuccino," said Beulah Jean. "Otherwise, you'll need to carry me out."

"My pleasure," said Jack giving her a kiss on the cheek. "I'll carry you anywhere. How about a drive up the coast tomorrow? Maybe the fresh sea air will help you sort out those dead body facts. We could make a day of it. I've been wanting to see what Ocean Isle Beach has to offer."

"I do have some thoughts I'd like to bounce off you.

Maybe getting out on the beach will clear my head for the next phase of my investigation. You've sold me."

Chapter Six

Before they left for Ocean Isle Beach, they dropped Miss Shelby off at the veterinary clinic for her annual check-up, and Beulah Jean convinced Jack to stop at the mall. She thought his take on the merchants who hired her would be helpful if they were going to dissect the case later that day.

Brandy Sommers was standing on a step ladder placing colorful sea glass birds on the top shelf of a display in the window of her store. When she saw Beulah Jean, she pointed to a box on the counter in the middle of the room.

"I put aside a few samples of the sea glass the police detectives are referring to in their latest theory," she said stepping down from the ladder. "Maybe you can convince them these are of a much superior quality to the piece they are carrying around. The one they found in the dead man's hand."

Beulah Jean had read the latest information sent from Detective Collins when she and Jack returned home the night before from Maggi Ds. They discussed the sea glass mentioned in the report and wondered about the connection to Ms. Sommers and her merchandise.

"Have they seen these samples?" asked Beulah Jean.

"Not a one," said Brandy. "They came and interviewed me the day the body was discovered, but never touched a piece of glass. "After they called last night with the accusation that I might be responsible for the man's death, I came in early this morning and pulled these samples. You can see how the designs in the pieces are one of a kind. These are not even considered to be in the same ballpark as the thick green glass they described over the phone. They're planning to stop by later this morning. I'm so glad you came in. I was going to call you when I finished my display."

Jack had picked up a couple of pieces from the box. "These are much lighter than I would have thought," he said holding a piece between his forefinger and thumb, rubbing it gently. "Not as thick as I would have guessed."

Beulah Jean walked around the store looking for anything that resembled the sea glass she had seen on the beach. "Much of your glass is red and orange. Are those colors harder to find?"

"The red sea glass has always been rare because of how

it's made," said Brandy. "Some red glass is created by using particles of gold. If you find a red piece of glass, it most likely came from an old Schlitz beer bottle. Collectors search out orange sea glass. It's the rarest color because there was very little orange glass made."

Beulah Jean remembered the report from Detective Collins which mentioned that the glass found in the dead man's hand was green. "How rare was the piece they have in evidence?" she asked Brandy.

"The most commonly found colors are green, brown and white. This doesn't mean all glass in those colors are common. The thickness and age will play a part in the determination of value. The piece the detective described last night on the phone seemed pretty common. I'll know better when I see it."

"If you can identify the piece as one you would have had in your inventory, please call me after they leave. My instinct tells me they are riding on a little wishful thinking."

Beulah Jean and Jack headed for the Olive Shop. She wanted Jack to meet the other two merchants whose names she was asked to clear.

"What a nice surprise," said Ellen O'Connell when she

saw Beulah Jean. "Do you have good news? Tell me they found the person responsible for the dead man."

"Afraid not. They seem to have their eyes on your friend Brandy."

"I'm not surprised. As soon as she told me she was here early the morning he was found, I was sure they would make her a prime suspect."

"I don't think it has anything to do with the time she arrived," said Beulah Jean. She didn't feel the sea glass found in the victim's hand was common knowledge. And hearing that news from another merchant would be far superior to hearing it from her. And there was that police code of honor.

"This is my friend, Jack. He's a detective on the Isle of Palms. I'm giving him a tour of the crime scene. Thought I would pick up another bottle of that Cranberry Pear Olive Oil for him to take back home."

"Great," said Ellen. "I have only two bottles of that flavor left. They have flown off the shelves. Guess I picked a winner." She wrapped the bottle in specially coated brown paper and placed it in a bag.

"I'll have a new shipment here by the time you finish

this bottle."

"Thanks, Ellen. I wanted to show Jack where they found that woman's body last month. Do you have a moment to come out back with us?"

Ellen called over to her assistant and asked her to take charge while they were out of the shop. "We can use my back door. The crime scene is a few feet from my exit. That's why the Myrtle Beach detectives keep watch, hoping I'll give them a reason to arrest me."

Jack and Beulah Jean followed Ellen to the spot where the woman was found. There were still CSI markers in the area. Each had a number. There would be something in the report describing what every number meant.

Beulah Jean took pictures so she could match the report to the site markings when she got back to her office. Jack asked Ellen several questions about the position of the body and the surrounding area before he nodded his completion to Beulah Jean. She asked Ellen to call Dan Logan to let him know they were on their way to his store. As they turned the corner in the mall to the area where the Kitchen Cutlery was located, Jack began asking questions.

"So, I understand the connection to Brandy's sea glass,

and the location to Ellen's shop," said Jack. "But why is this guy a person of interest to the Myrtle Beach Police Department?"

"Dan told me they wanted to examine two of his display cases. The ones with the serrated knives and the professional Hollow Edge Knives. There was also a velvet-lined box in the case with a few cutting knives for carving."

"Was the woman cut anywhere on her body?" asked Jack.

"I didn't read anything about any blood or cuts in her case file."

"There must be some reason they put him on their list."

Beulah Jean tried to remember what the connection might be as they arrived at the door to the Kitchen Cutlery. Everything was closed up and a sign on the door read: *CLOSED FOR VACATION. RETURNING NEXT WEEK.*

"This is strange, Jack." She called Ellen from her cell phone.

"Did you know Dan was away on vacation?" she asked when Ellen answered.

"He never said anything to me. He didn't answer his cell when I called. Did you ask the clerk he left in charge?"

"The shop is closed. Locked up tight. It seems no one is in charge. The sign says he's on vacation."

"I don't understand," said Ellen. "He was on vacation two weeks ago. Left his assistant in charge. I saw him a couple days ago. With you, as a matter of fact. He said nothing about going out of town. I haven't spoken to him in the last twenty-four hours."

"Well, something caused him to close his shop," said Beulah Jean. "If you hear anything, please call me. I'll talk to you later."

Jack and Beulah Jean walked through the mall before getting in their car and heading for Ocean Isle Beach. She wanted him to get the lay of the land so he would understand things when she talked about her findings.

The ride up Route 17 North was crowded until they got to the North Carolina line. They decided to take Route 179 in Calabash and follow it to the rotary that led to Ocean Isle Beach. Once they crossed the Intracoastal Waterway, they lowered the windows and inhaled the salty ocean air. Looking north they could see canal after canal lined with two story beach cottages, each with a dock for fishing, and most with a boat at the ready. Off the first roundabout, there were white tents housing vendors with offerings of arts and crafts. Jack parked the car in the public lot, and they walked through a passageway toward the warm sand along the shore.

"It's been a while since we walked on the sand," said Beulah Jean as she removed her sandals and pressed her bare feet into the space left by a small wave as the water rippled out to sea. Jack followed suit and they laughed at the different size of each impression.

"For a detective who exudes such authority, you sure have small feet," said Jack. "Probably the only bare part of your body I've never noticed before."

"Whoa there, Detective Handy. This is supposed to be a working session. I need to stay in a professional mode right now. Don't tell me you're backing out of your commitment."

"I've never been able to remain in a professional mode with you for longer than a few minutes. And these surroundings sure don't support your request. But let's give it a try."

Beulah Jean was sure Jack was referring to the bikini-clad females walking along the water's edge. It was time to change his focus.

"Any thoughts on last month's crime scene outside the Olive Shop?" she asked as she took his hand and led him along the shoreline.

"It looks like a great place for the homeless to use when the weather is less than ideal. Did the Myrtle Beach detectives question any homeless groups for clues?"

"The reports I read had some information from the usual homeless hangouts. I do want to check out the trailer parks a few blocks away from the mall. I'm hoping someone has seen something that could lead me toward a working theory," said Beulah Jean. "There's only ten days left on the woman's case before they send her body to SLED for the final thirty before they give up and dispose of her."

"It's clear they're following the South Carolina protocol?"

"Seems like every T is crossed, and I dotted with that case," said Beulah Jean.

"There's got to be something we're missing. A woman doesn't just go missing and die without someone looking for her."

"If she was homeless," said Jack working a theory, "She could have recently arrived in Myrtle Beach and hadn't met anyone before she was taken to the backside of the mall. Did you note any similarities between the two bodies?"

"Well, they both were shoeless. However, neither of them looked like the typical homeless person - the ones who hardly get to shower and shave. I didn't get the feeling either of the bodies belonged to people who were on the streets very long. The clothes looked like they came from a department store, appeared clean and probably hadn't been on the bodies long before they were found dead."

"Did either of them have any identifying marks, like tattoos or scars?"

"Nothing was noted on paper," said Beulah Jean. The picture of the woman I saw in the files didn't say homeless. Her hair was chin length, very smooth and even highlighted. Not something a homeless woman could afford. And the man's face had a dark shadow with no visible tattoos. His hair couldn't have had more than a few weeks' growth. Neither of them would be mistaken for a member of the homeless population."

"So, the man had sea glass in his hand," said Jack. "Did the woman have any cuts or blood on her?"

"She had a few scrapes on her elbows and heels. The Myrtle Beach detectives attributed them to being dragged a few feet before she was left on the ground."

"I'm still trying to figure how Dan's knives might fit into the picture," said Jack.

Beulah Jean's cell phone rang. She pulled it from the back pocket of her jeans.

"Hey Doug, I was going to call you later this afternoon," she said stepping away from the waves hitting her ankles and moving onto the dry sand. "Do you have a reason for me to put a period on the end of this case?"

"Sorry, no. But you remember your suggestion to check the inside of the man's wedding ring for an inscription?"

"Anything?"

"Might be our first real lead on John Doe."

Chapter Seven

"Anything you want to share?" Jack asked when Beulah Jean caught up with him at the edge of the water.

"Not sure it means much. The inscription on the inside of the dead man's ring said: *Bonnie Forever 10-10-10.* I'm assuming Bonnie was his wife, and they either got married on that date, or she died in 2010."

"How old do you think the dead guy was?" asked Jack.

"Maybe mid-to-late thirties." Beulah Jean did the math in her head. "Has to be a wedding date. Otherwise, she would have died as a married teen."

"If that's the case, why hasn't she filed a missing person's report?"

"Maybe she doesn't know he came to Myrtle Beach. He could be from anywhere. The Chamber of Commerce has an amazing public relations campaign. My aunt saw an ad for this place when she was vacationing in Maine last year."

They walked along the shore in silence for nearly ten minutes before they came to the end of the beach houses where several feet of sand had been added to the shoreline. They stood looking out to sea, deep in their own theories.

"Penny for your thoughts," said Jack.

Beulah Jean realized she had stopped moving. "I've been thinking about the merchants at the mall looking for me to clear their names. Wondering if olive oil, knives or sea glass could be connected to these murders?"

"My guess would be one of the latter two," said Jack. "Never heard of olive oil killing anyone. In fact, I think it's known for healing."

"I'm going to look into that green sea glass found in the dead man's hand. The small cut on the palm of his hand surely couldn't have killed him. Even so, the fact that he was holding the glass makes me wonder why. Could someone have moved him from the beach into the mall after he was dead? Seems pretty hard to believe."

"I agree," said Jack. "Was there any beach sand around his body?"

"None that I'm aware of. I'll check further, but I don't remember any mention of sand on the floor near the body."

She drew a heart in the sand with her toes and watched as a small wave washed it away.

"My mind has been working the knives theory," said Jack, "Your Kitchen Cutlery owner."

"Okay, let's go there for a minute. Neither body showed any apparent cuts. How do you see knives playing a part in either death?"

"I don't. That's the problem. But why has he closed his shop and gone on vacation? He knows the investigation is in high gear. Doesn't make sense for him to leave now? I've been trying to understand why he asked you to clear his name in the first place."

"Dan told me the detectives kept coming back to him with more questions. I didn't get any details on the kinds of questions they were asking. I'll have to do a deep dive into the woman's case. Maybe we can review it together tonight when we get back to Market Common."

"I'm all yours," said Jack. "Let's walk back to the car and find a place to grab some lunch before we head home."

They stopped at the Ocean Isle Fish Company. Their table on the Tiki Bar's upper deck overlooked all of Ocean Isle Beach, the marsh, and the Atlantic Ocean. They saw the fishermen onloading their catch at the dock as the island music added the perfect atmosphere for a relaxed lunch.

"I'll have a Pina Colada," said Beulah Jean when the waitress arrived at their table.

"Make mine a frozen marguerita with salt," said Jack. "And we'll have the lobster and shrimp nachos for two."

"Sounds delish," she whispered as the waitress walked away. "How did you know that would be my choice?"

"I'm a detective. Besides after nearly a year in your company I think I can read your mind."

"Is that right? Well, what is my mind telling you about my latest investigation?"

"Nothing good. I think I'm in for a lot of long lonely commutes back to the Isle of Palms. Feels like you're gonna hunker down in the Myrtle Beach area searching for clues."

"I think you really can read my mind," said Beulah Jean leaning over and kissing him on the cheek. "I'm sorry this case is cramping your style. I'm clueless right now and it's frustrating."

"Been there," said Jack. "It's been a while, but I remember how that feels. I'm just glad you're able to share your thoughts with me. I want to help. Let's review all those files tonight and see if two minds can find any headway."

"That's why you're a keeper," she said kissing his cheek again.

"Continue with this and I might have to stop on the way home and get a room."

She knew this was not the right time to admit her feelings. Their relationship had grown over the last few months, and she couldn't imagine life without him by her side. Their food arrived and broke her train of thought.

The drive south took longer than expected and the veterinary clinic was about to close for the day when they arrived. Miss Shelby nearly jumped into Beulah Jean's arms when she saw her. In addition to her annual physical, she had been pampered with their bathing and brushing services. She looked like a beautifully mature golden retriever - gray face and all.

"Sorry Girl," said Beulah Jean. "The traffic slowed us down, but we would never have left you here overnight."

"Here's the report on her wellness check," said the Vet Tech. "She's doing well for an old girl. See you in six months."

The dog snuggled close, and Beulah Jean could feel Miss Shelby's tail hitting her leg all the way out to the car.

When they got back to her townhouse, Beulah Jean and Jack spent hours going over all the information in the files from both mall deaths. Miss Shelby planted herself on Beulah Jean's left foot under the table and slept the night away.

Jack had taken enough notes to fill two pages of questions. "Did you say the detectives took a picture of the dead woman over to the soup kitchen?"

"I think so. It should be in the blue file in that box marked *Jane Doe.*"

"It's pretty generic. A crime scene photo never does justice," said Jack. "It would really help to have a picture from an event in her life. I'm not surprised she hasn't been identified from this version."

"You're right. But it's all they have. I might not even show this picture to people I speak with at the trailer park. Maybe a description of a thirty-something woman with medium length highlighted hair would garner more response."

Jack looked down at his notebook. "I'm having trouble

with the bare feet. Did they find shoes anywhere near the body?"

"Nothing in the report. There is a note attesting to the condition of her feet. Says they were not dirty and didn't appear walked on for any distance. She had a few scrapes on her elbows and heals, and the edges of her pants had a few tears, like she had been dragged and left. Maybe even carried to that spot where she was found."

"When I looked outside the Olive Shop, the ground was mostly cement. Any reference to the CSI numbers on the ground?"

"There is something here," said Beulah Jean. "Number 4: Blue fiber matching woman's pants."

"According to the pictures I took with my iPhone, looks like Number 4 was close to the opening out to the parking lot," said Jack. "Were any numbers placed in the lot?"

"Not anywhere in these notes," said Beulah Jean. Wonder if they did a sweep out there? Number 2 notes refer to some wood shavings by the back door. Did you notice a chunk of wood missing anywhere?"

"I never checked out the building for any clues, only the ground where the body was found. We should probably go back and take more pictures. There are so few leads in this case. You might have to start looking down rabbit holes."

"Not sure why I've looked at this like the two were related. I'm going to have to start treating each case on its own merits, or lack thereof." She pulled out an easel from behind the door and ripped off the top sheet of paper on the pad that sat in the holder. With a black magic marker, she began listing the facts she had collected on the woman's death.

"No name, no other identification, no one reported a missing person fitting her description. Mid-thirties, highlighted hair, manicured nails, no signs of homelessness. This is going nowhere fast. Quite the mystery."

Jack stared at her notes resting on the easel. "A nearly perfect one at that."

They decided to take a break and enjoy some wine and cheese. Beulah Jean had planned to make Jack dinner, but he had other plans. By the time they were ready to continue going over the facts of the case, it was nearly midnight.

Chapter Eight

Monday morning came fast. The entire weekend was spent going over all the information Beulah Jean had pulled together for Jack's input. When he left for the Isle of Palms, she promised him her goal for the coming week was to move closer to solving the mystery of the dead woman in order to clear her clients' names. That would mean she could spend time at Jack's place next weekend. She loved cruising on the Intracoastal Waterway in his boat.

She watered and fed Miss Shelby and headed out for the trailer park near the mall. She quickly discovered there was more than one – in fact, there were several. She began knocking on doors at the first trailer after the entrance to Myrtle Rest.

"Have you seen this woman," she asked the Hispanic female in her early twenties who came to the door with a baby in her arms. "She would have been in the area last month."

"No, ma'am. "I don't get outside much. My baby has been sick, and he can't be in the sun. The woman at the end of the lane is always walking in the neighborhood. She might have seen that person."

Beulah Jean thanked her and then drove to the end of the road being careful going over the speed bumps. She didn't see anyone sitting outside along the way and, wondered if anyone was home during the day. She parked her powder blue VW bug in front of a double wide and knocked on the door. No answer. She got back into her convertible and drove around until she found herself back out on Route 15. There was a gas station and convenient store a few blocks north. She decided to try her luck with the clerk at the counter.

"I was wondering if you would let me hang this information on your bulletin board," she asked, handing her a business card. "I'm hoping someone might have seen this woman around here last month."

The clerk looked closely at the picture. "I don't remember anyone looking like her. You're welcome to post it on the board."

"Thanks. I'm not having any luck. There are more

trailer parks in this area than I was aware of. I haven't even seen many people outside. Do most of these residents live here year-round? Are there any vacation areas nearby?"

"In the immediate area, most of these people are permanent residents. There are a lot more vacation trailers a few streets down at the KOA campgrounds. There are permanent campers and RVs that are mostly used as vacation spots. You could try your luck there." Beulah Jean thanked her and asked for specific directions to the site.

She stopped at the entrance to the KOA Campgrounds and went into the office.

"I'm Beulah Jean Pickens, a private investigator," showing the woman her badge. "I'm looking for a missing person." She showed the desk clerk the picture she had of the dead woman. "She would have been in this area last month. I was hoping someone in the campgrounds might have seen her."

The clerk took out a map of the facility and showed Beulah Jean the campground specifics. "This area is set up for people who bring their own tents. They usually don't stay for more than a week. Then we have this area set aside for people who want a site to hook up their fifth wheel or

RV. Some of those people stay a few weeks, normally not more than a month. Your best bet would be to drive out back by this road. There are about sixty sites with permanent trailers. They rent by the month or year. Most of them are annual rentals. Some owners have been here over ten years. They come for months at a time. Some spend the summer. Some are snowbirds. They have friends or relatives who come to use their trailer for days or weeks at a time. We don't know every time someone visits. You might have better luck back in that area. That picture doesn't look like any of our permanent residents. Most of them look older than she appears. Maybe someone in the permanent back lot saw her."

"Thanks. You've been very helpful. I'll drive back there and ask around."

Beulah Jean was anxious to test out her theory. This dead woman had to be seen by someone. She decided to put away her photo and just describe the woman.

She parked next to someone's fenced in patio. It was obvious no one was there. She hoped she would have a few hours before they returned. The dirt roads were short but there were close to twenty of them along the backside of the property. She walked three streets before she saw the man sitting with a book in his hands at an umbrella table on his patio.

"Excuse me, sir," she said to the sixty-something male with all his hair growing down from his chin and nothing on the top of his head. "I'm a private investigator looking for a missing person. I wonder if I could ask you a few questions?"

He looked up from his book. That's when she noticed his eyebrows were bushy and might cover his forehead if brushed upward. "What can I do for you, ma'am?"

"Have you been at this site for a long time?"

"I spend five months of each year enjoying these surroundings, along with maybe a third of the occupants."

"Last month a young woman went missing and it seems no one has seen her. She was in her mid-thirties with light brown hair sprinkled with streaks of blond. Do you remember seeing anyone like her in this area?"

"My eyesight's not that good. That's why I'm reading this large print mystery. But a young woman like that, well, I'm sure I would have noticed. Most of us are retired. The younger folk usually stay in the section up front. Many are on vacation. Did you ask Helen over on Birch Lane?" he said pointing off to the right. "She plans a lot of activities for us older owners."

"I haven't been up that way yet. Thank you for your help. Helen, you said?"

"Yes. She has the best grass in her side yard. Very welcoming. Someone might have mentioned something to her about a younger woman."

She walked toward the area the old man described. Just before she got to the yard he referred to, she passed a woman sitting in a swing in the shade of her property. Her nearly white curly hair reminded Beulah Jean of her aunt who always got a perm in the hot weather.

"Excuse me, ma'am," she said. "I wonder if I could ask you a few questions."

"We don't allow soliciting in this area," she said putting down her knitting needles. "The management is very strict about that."

"I'm a private investigator looking for a missing person. I wondered if you might have seen her."

"We don't get a lot of strangers back here. We're all

owners. Not many visitors."

"This woman might have been a visitor. She was in her mid-thirties with kind of a bob haircut with several highlights." Beulah Jean hoped this woman would understand her description better than the photo she had in her purse.

"Well. There was someone a few weeks back could fit that description. She was staying in Marsha's fifth wheel. She isn't here now. Said she was going back to her husband if it's the woman I'm remembering."

Beulah Jean could feel the hair on her arms standing at attention.

"So, you spoke with the woman, Mrs…?" Beulah Jean realized she didn't ask the woman's name.

"Oh. I'm Dorothy Clarkson. Yes. Marsha's place is the one on the other side of this RV next to me. The Harrisons have gone to visit their daughter. She just had a baby earlier than expected. Marsha never had time to tell me about her visitor. Bernice would walk down to the beach every day. Sometimes she would stop on her way back to her trailer."

"What can you tell me about Bernice?"

"She was not real happy. Cute little thing. Said she left

her husband and was trying to decide whether she should get a divorce."

"Did she tell you where she was from or what she did for a living?"

"She was a potter. Showed me a picture one afternoon of some of her works. Everything looked very professional and expensive. Even some unusual jewelry. She had her own shop in North Carolina. Said she shut things up and came to the beach."

"Did she say where in North Carolina?"

"It was somewhere along that pottery trail in Seagrove. I went there once with my husband before he passed. There must be a couple hundred artists along that highway."

"Did Bernice ever tell you her last name?"

"No ma'am. And I never asked. She seemed so sad. I hope she is back with her husband. Their marriage was not in great shape when she left. I think he might have been into drugs or alcohol. She never really said."

"Thank you for the information. You've been very helpful. Would you happen to have a phone number for the Harrisons? Maybe I can find out more about Bernice."

"I don't, but the manager up in the office should have

one."

Beulah Jean nearly ran back to her car. This was the first bit of information she thought might lead to the dead woman. The office was closed. She took down the phone number on the door and decided to call when she got back to her office.

Miss Shelby was excited as usual to see her owner. She started doing figure eights through Beulah Jean's legs. Something she did since she was a pup. She went outside but did her business quickly. Getting that treat when she returned to the office was always her priority.

Beulah Jean opened her laptop and started typing up as much as she could remember from her visit to the campground. When she finished, she called the number on the door of the campground office. She could hardly wait for someone to answer.

"Hi. This is Beulah Jean Pickens, the private investigator. I spoke with you this morning."

"Yes. Did you have any luck with our owners?"

"I think so. Would you happen to have a phone number

for the Harrisons?" The woman two trailers down the road said someone stayed in their trailer a few weeks ago. I was hoping to call them."

"I'm sorry. It's our policy not to give out phone numbers of our residents. I could try to contact them and give them your information."

"Well. Anything would help at this point. Yes. You have my card. Please give them my number and let them know it's very important. Especially if they haven't been in touch with their niece recently."

"I will call them and give them your message."

"Thanks." Beulah Jean was not convinced. Could be her experience with people not wanting to talk with private investigators. She hit the red dot on her iPhone and immediately called Detective Collins.

"Hey. It's Beulah Jean. I think I have something."

Chapter Nine

"I'm all ears," said Detective Collins.

"I spent a good part of today scouting the campgrounds behind the mall," said Beulah Jean.

"My men checked out a few places back there," said Collins, but had no luck. They spent two solid weeks at the soup kitchen. Nothing."

"Well, I can't swear to it, but I think I have a credible lead to the dead woman. She could be from North Carolina according to a Mrs. Clarkson, one of the residents of the KOA Campground. Said she spoke with her several times. Thinks she went back to her husband. She was staying in a fifth wheel two sites down the road."

"Did you get her information?"

"Only a first name - Bernice. A potter, possibly from the Seagrove area of North Carolina. There's a trail of several miles of pottery shops in that town according to Clarkson. The manager at the campsite wouldn't break policy. She said she would call and give them my number. Nothing yet."

"Well let's not wait long. If you haven't heard by morning, I'll send my investigators over. Keep me posted."

"Will do. Tell me about the wood shavings on the ground near the dead woman," asked Beulah Jean. "It's described under item #2 in the crime scene report. Is there any more to that story?"

"Let me take a look," said Collins.

Beulah Jean used the time to look through the report for the notes about the other markings on the ground outside the Olive Shop.

"I have a handwritten scribble next to that #2 marking," said Collins. Looks like it says there were no cuts in the fencing to account for the shavings. There's a double question mark after the comment. I'll have to ask Detectives Stone and Wexler what they meant by that finding."

"And what about the marking noting the blue fiber matching the woman's pants?"

"Looks like we had a piece of the hem in the evidence locker. I'm not sure if we still have it in house or if it's been sent ahead with the corpse."

"So, there was a rip of some kind?"

"I think they determined the body was dragged along the

cement. Says her heels were scraped. Could have torn a piece of the hem. Most likely in the parking lot on the way into the area where the body was found."

"Maybe the shoes came off when the body was being moved," said Beulah Jean. "They didn't find any shoes in the parking lot?"

"Not according to the notes or the contents of the evidence locker."

"Before I let you go…. can you give me any insight into why the owner of the Kitchen Cutlery store is a person of interest?"

"My guys followed him for a few days after they saw him coming out of the soup kitchen. They thought he might have known the woman and was trying to cover up any loose ends he could have left."

"Did they come up empty or is he still on the person of interest list?"

"Stone told me yesterday they were about to clear him until he left town for the second time in a couple of weeks. There inquiring about his current whereabouts."

"I did see a sign on his shop door, yesterday. I've never seen a store in a mall closing for vacation. Usually they get coverage." Beulah Jean was hoping to get a lead on where Dan might have gone.

"That's exactly why we're still watching him. Very unusual behavior."

Beulah Jean's iPhone beeped, and she could see she had another call waiting. "This could be the campground manager calling. Let me call you back."

"Let's hope it's good news."

She hit the new caller mark. "Good afternoon, Pickens Investigations."

"Detective Pickens, this is Eva, the manager at the KOA Campgrounds."

"Yes, Eva. Did you reach the Harrisons?"

"I did call, but there was no answer. And when I tried to leave a message, the recording said the mailbox was full. I will try again tomorrow and hope they have checked their messages and deleted enough to make room for more."

"That's not good news," said Beulah Jean. "We're trying to identify a dead body and there seems to be a resemblance to the Harrisons' visitor."

"Oh no," said Eva. "I hope you're wrong. The Harrisons are lovely people. I'll ask around to see if anyone has any other number for them."

"Thanks. Please keep me posted," said Beulah Jean. She hung up and sat staring out the window. Miss Shelby woke up and shook off two hours of sleep. She got to her dish before Beulah Jean could fill it with the special diet food the vet prescribed for delicate stomachs. She sat next to her dog on the floor and stared out into the backyard. There had to be something she could do to move this investigation along. If she could get a confirmation of the Harrisons' visitor, she could take that lead and run with it. Right now, she was at another dead end.

The phone rang and caused her to jump up. She leaned over toward her desk and answered.

"Beulah Jean, it's Doug Collins. Thought you were going to call me back."

"Sorry. I got sidetracked. The manager at the campground says there was no answer, and her voicemail box is full. She's looking through her files for any other contact information."

"I could send my detectives over there, but they might not get any further. If you don't have anything by morning, I'll get a warrant to search the Harrisons' trailer. My guys might find something to lead us to her visitor."

"I suppose that's an option. I'm not feeling good about getting through to the Harrisons. I meant to ask before. Did your men bring that green sea glass over to Brandy Sommers at Seaside Treasurers?"

"They got tied up but are planning to go there tonight."

"Mind if I attend the meeting?"

"No. She's one of your clients on this case, isn't she?"

"Yes. I was there on Saturday. She showed me what she had set out for your men to examine. Didn't look like what they were describing from the dead man's hand. I need something else to untangle right now. My mind is a boggle. Solving anything at this point will be a win."

"Be my guest. Hope you come up a winner."

Detectives Stone and Wexler were already at the Seaside Treasures' glass counter talking to Brandy Sommers when Beulah Jean arrived. She could hear things were tense as she approached the trio, engrossed in heavy conversation.

"Detective Pickens, please explain to these men the difference between their sea glass and my merchandise," said Brandy. "I can't seem to get anywhere with them."

"Good evening, detectives," said Beulah Jean. She looked at the sea glass Stone was holding. "I'm not much of a sea glass connoisseur either, but since I spoke with Brandy on Saturday, I've done a little research." She took a piece of glass Brandy had placed in a tray to show the detectives.

"One of the signs of perfection is the thickness of the glass." She held the piece between her thumb and forefinger and brought it up to their eye level. Then she asked if she could hold the piece they had up next to hers. "You can see clearly the one you took from the dead man's hand is much thicker. Indicative of the more common findings along the beach."

Both men nodded in agreement. Then Detective Stone picked another piece from Brandy's tray. "This piece is as thick as the one we brought," he said.

"Yes, but it's red. A much more valuable piece," explained Brandy.

"Brandy, do you have the name of an expert who could look at the piece found on the man?" asked Beulah Jean.

Brandy looked in a jeweled box on the shelf under the counter and pulled out a business card. "This is the man I hire when I'm unsure of the value of a piece of sea glass. He has an office in Charleston. I'm sure he'd be able to identify exactly where that glass is usually found."

Beulah Jean could see the detectives were not biting. "I think it could be valuable," she told them. "If nothing else, they might have a lead as to where in Myrtle Beach this man was hanging out. Could narrow down the location along the more than fifty miles of beach on the grand strand."

Stone took the business card. "I suppose we could try one more wild goose chase," he said. The two men turned and started for the store exit.

"Speaking of chases, detectives, could I speak with you outside?" asked Beulah Jean. She turned back to Brandy. "Let's hope your glass expert will keep these guys away from here."

"Thanks Detective Pickens. I'm glad you suggested calling him. Maybe I can finally get a good night's sleep."

"I'm no glass expert," said Beulah Jean. "But I don't think that glass would ever be found on your shelves. I'll talk with you when they confirm my opinion."

She walked out into the mall and caught up with Stone and Wexler.

"I didn't want to ask in front of Brandy, but have you got any new information on the owner of the Kitchen Cutlery?"

"We have a copy of a plane ticket to Texas," said Wexler.

"Texas? Did you locate any relatives down there?"

"None. And the ticket is a one way. There's no return date."

"He's actually a client of mine," said Beulah Jean. "You'd think he would let me know when he leaves town in case I have information for him. Guess he's not that worried about clearing his name."

"We have a unit in Houston looking out for him. If we hear anything we'll pass it on."

"Thanks." She started to leave the mall but decided to walk by Dan's shop to see if there was anyone running the store.

She could tell as soon as she turned the corner there were no lights coming from inside the Kitchen Cutlery. Maybe there would be a new note announcing when the store would re-open. Nothing on the door at all. The original note was gone.

She leaned in and tried to see inside.

"You're the detective working for some of our merchants," said a forty-something woman with red hair piled on top of her head who walked up beside Beulah Jean. "She wore frameless glasses and her nametag said Margie Kane.

"Yes," said Beulah Jean. "Are you from the management office?"

"God, no. I'm the manager of the fragrance and lotions counter at Dowds Department Store. I'm Margie."

"So how did you know I was hired by some of the merchants?"

"I guess I know pretty much everything that goes on in this building. It's kind of a hobby of mine."

Beulah Jean had met a few 'Mrs. Kravitz-like' women before. They usually get in her way. However, sometimes they can share the exact piece of missing information.

"Nice to meet you, Margie. I'm Investigator Pickens. Do you know who's responsible for the dead man and woman?"

"Not yet. Working all my usual contacts. I know that woman was no homeless person."

"What makes you so sure?"

"No one with a manicure, pedicure and professional highlights in her hair would ever be mistaken for homeless."

"You sure about the nails?"

"Both painted 'Spring Fling' by OPI. I know my products."

"Who told you they were painted?"

"Saw them myself. A bunch of us went out to the parking lot when they were putting her in the coroner's van. As they moved her inside the zipper opened when they scraped the left side of the body bag. Her hand fell outside the bag. I could see the color clearly."

Beulah Jean decided this woman could just be the extra eyes she needed on this case.

"You wouldn't happen to know where the owner of this cutlery shop would be?"

"That's why I'm here right now. I think he's gone for more than a few days. I wouldn't be surprised if he didn't return."

"Do you have any solid evidence to support your theory?"

"Let's just call it intuition. I'm still working the details."

Beulah Jean handed Margie a business card. "Please call me when your evidence proves solid. Or anything else you find out regarding the two bodies."

"You'll be the first call I make," she said.

Beulah Jean couldn't wait to get home and call Jack.

Chapter Ten

He answered before the second ring. "I was just thinking about you," said Jack. "Wondering if you were planning to spend the night at the trailer park."

"If I thought sleeping there would get me the answers I need, I would."

"Sounds like you had a bad day."

Holding the cell phone up to her ear, Beulah Jean took her hot cup of decaf from the Keurig machine and sat down in her living room. "Actually, I might have had a good day. The verdict is still out."

"If there anything I can do to tilt the scale?"

"Not from this distance. Hearing your voice helps. My frustration is causing me to spin. Even Miss Shelby is pacing back and forth. She knows what I'm like when I'm waiting for something out of my control."

"So, if I'm reading you correctly, the right phone call

can do the trick?"

"Right."

"And it's not mine."

"Sorry. I really need to hear from the manager at the KOA Campgrounds. I spoke to a summer resident who believes she was talking to the woman found dead last month. The problem is, she only knows her first name, and the trailer she was staying in belongs to a couple no one can reach. To make matters worse, they don't even know people are trying to get in touch with them because their voice mailbox is full. Detective Collins is standing by to bring a search warrant over there. I'm not convinced he'll find out anything I don't already know."

"Well, what do you know?" asked Jack.

"I spoke with a Mrs. Clarkson. She was sitting outside on her patio. She said a young woman fitting the description I gave her was staying in a trailer a few doors away. Said her name was Bernice and, is a potter who has a shop along the pottery trail near Seagrove, North Carolina."

"Sounds like a pretty good lead to me."

"No last name. No address or phone number," she rambled on.

"When has that ever stopped you?"

"Seagrove is more than three hours away. Not sure I'm up for searching for a needle in that haystack. Could come up empty-handed."

"How 'bout we take a couple of days and drive north? We could make it a little nicer by exploring the area and staying overnight."

"You'd do that for me?"

"That's the least of what I'd do for you. I haven't taken any of the time I banked last year. We could actually stay away for a month."

Beulah Jean could feel her body relaxing. The idea of having another detective on the case reminded her of all the times she worked with Adam before he died. Even though she promised herself she'd never work with a partner again, Jack's offer opened that door a crack.

"Let's save some of that unused vacation for when this mystery is solved. A few days should be more than enough time to check out this Bernice character. I'd love to have your mind on this case with me."

"I was hoping you'd want more of me than my mind."

Beulah Jean loved how they bantered about being

together. She knew how he felt about her. Soon she would make sure he knew how she felt about him.

"How soon can you get away from the island?"

"I only need a day to finish a couple reports from my last case. I'll let them know tomorrow that I'll be taking time away. Why don't I drive up after work and we can leave the next morning?"

"Sounds like a plan. I'll let Detective Collins know I'll be out of town in case he gets any other leads while I'm gone. Now let me tell you about my latest 'Gossip Girl.' She couldn't wait to let me know how she's working my case."

"The last time I had someone offer her services she turned out to be covering up for the thief," said Jack. "Let me get a beer and take it out on the dock. Then I'm all ears."

Miss Shelby nearly knocked over Beulah Jean as she tried to maneuver her way into the back seat of Jack's car. She quickly moved to her favorite spot and settled down for the morning ride to Seagrove, North Carolina. Traffic on route

501 North was slowed to a stop near the technical college. Across the street, the church was selling pumpkins and there was a line of cars trying to exit into the parking lot.

"The GPS says we should be on that pottery trail in about three hours," said Jack. "The internet says we're going to America's largest community of working potters."

"You certainly have done your homework," said Beulah Jean. "Let's hope this effort pays off."

"I have every confidence in your ability to find Bernice. Whatever her last name is. I know Detective Collins is counting on you. Especially after your last phone call with him this morning."

"I told him his men probably won't get anywhere by searching that trailer. People don't keep their vital information in a vacation trailer. And if that Bernice stayed there, I doubt she left a trail. The fact that the Harrisons haven't cleared their messages on their phone only confirms my need to make this trip. We might find something before they do."

"Detectives Stone and Wexler might be able to get a DNA sample of hair from a brush," said Jack. Or some fingerprints they could match to the dead woman."

"I suppose anything's possible. I'm not counting on them. My mind is focused on finding Bernice." She took out her cell phone and started searching for potters in Seagrove. "Crap. There are forty-nine pottery shops and four pottery galleries on that trail. I'm glad we took clothes for an overnight stay."

"While you were on the phone with Detective Collins this morning, I made a reservation for us at the pet friendly Hampton Inn and Suites in Asheboro. There's a brewery in the town and a couple of restaurants that look promising."

"Now there's the Jack I know and love."

Jack slowed the car and pulled off 501 into the parking lot of a bird house shop in Aynor.

"Could you say that out loud one more time?" he asked staring into her eyes.

Beulah Jean realized she might have tipped her hand.

"Yes. I said love. I thought you knew how I felt?"

"Let's say I was hopeful. Not really sure." He put her face in his hands and kissed her long and hard on her lips.

"Detective Handy, we are on a case that needs our complete attention. We should be on our way."

"You're right Investigator Pickens. I'm on it. But I'll

need some of that attention this evening." He pulled out of the parking lot and continued driving north.

Beulah Jean smiled and went back to searching on her iPhone. "Looks like a majority of the shops are on Route 705 off 220 in Seagrove. I think we should start there. No wait. There's a North Carolina Pottery Center. That's our first stop. Someone there should know where we could find the shop belonging to Bernice."

They spent the next two hours listening to music and enjoying the scenery. There was one stop for Miss Shelby to relieve herself, and time to purchase coffee for Jack and Beulah Jean.

They took Exit 61 off 220 and followed her iPhone directions to the Pottery Center and Museum on East Avenue. The woman at the counter informed them of the admission fee for the museum. Beulah Jean handed the woman her card and began her questioning.

"I'm Investigator Pickens and this is Detective Handy. We're looking for a woman who we believe owns one of the pottery shops on this trail. Would you have a directory of owners?"

"I'm Laura Randolph. This brochure lists each one of

our shops along with addresses and phone numbers. The owners' names are not listed, but I've worked here for nearly three years. I know most of the owners."

Beulah Jean looked at the brochure. Definitely a haystack. "The woman's name is Bernice. She's around thirty years old. I'm told she's married and has her own shop here in this area."

"I don't know anyone by that name," said Ms. Randolph. Do you know the kind of pottery she makes?"

The brochure showed pictures next to each listing of the kinds of pottery made in that shop. Beulah Jean looked over the options hoping something would come to mind. Her eyes stopped at a picture displaying handmade shaped and polished gemstones placed in original sterling settings.

"I was told the woman made some jewelry." She pointed to the picture on the brochure. "Can you tell me who owns this shop?"

Laura Randolph looked at the picture. "Oh, that's Bonnie's shop. She's been on vacation for quite a while. I'm not sure if she's back yet."

Beulah Jean looked at Jack. *Bonnie Forever 10-10-10*. She could tell he knew she was referring to the inscription on the wedding ring found on the dead man in the mall.

Chapter Eleven

Beulah Jean took a moment before she asked the most important question on her mind. She knew the answer could open up her entire case. In fact, both cases.

"I'd love to speak to her husband. Do you know if he would be at the shop? Or maybe you could give me their home address?"

There was a definite hesitation on the part of Laura Randolph. She looked around on her desk and appeared to be stalling before she answered the question.

"Scout has been out of town for several weeks. At least, no one around here has seen him. He's had a rough time adjusting to his return from Afghanistan. They're a great couple, but they've been trying to work out some issues with their marriage. Bonnie created beautiful pottery for years. Even when Scout was gone on his latest tour. But when he got back last fall things were difficult for them. She stopped working on new pieces. She would sit in her shop and sell her works for days without creating anything new. I saw Scout at the brewery a few times. Rumor has it, he was there a lot. We didn't see Bonnie at any of our regular gatherings and eventually we heard that they were talking divorce. Thank goodness they have no children."

"I'm sorry to hear that," said Beulah Jean. "And you say Bonnie has been on vacation?"

"Yes. She loves the Myrtle Beach area. Has gone there many times for a little R&R. I didn't see her before she left, but I'm sure she went toward the ocean. I hope she's getting the help she needs."

"What is Bonnie and Scout's last name?" asked Beulah Jean, going into her investigative mode. "And could I have their home address?"

"The Kramers live on the same property as Bonnie's shop. The dirt road splits a few feet off Route 705 near the Jugtown line. The house is set back from the two-room cottage she uses for a shop." She wrote down the address and handed it to Beulah Jean.

"What is the name of that brewery you mentioned?" asked Jack. "The one that Scout frequented?"

Beulah Jean knew Jack was working the cases with her.

"The Four Saints Brewing Company is actually up the road apiece," said Laura. "In Asheboro. You can't miss it if you drive north on Alternate 220."

"You've been very helpful," said Beulah Jean. "Can you direct me to your Police Department?"

"The office is two blocks away on East Main," said Laura. "Officer Griffin is our only fulltime police officer, so you might not find anyone there."

"I guess we really are out there in the country," said Beulah Jean. "Wish us luck," she said before she and Jack shook her hand and then walked out to their car."

Miss Shelby had been sleeping in the back seat but stood up when she heard them coming closer to the car.

"Will you walk her out by that field across the street, while I call Detective Collins," asked Beulah Jean.

"Way ahead of you," said Jack hooking Miss Shelby's leash to her collar. "Come on, girl."

Beulah Jean put her notes on the roof of the car and placed the call that she knew would open up both cases still pending.

"I was hoping to hear from you," said Detective Collins

when he heard who was calling. "I have an update on that trailer search."

"Great. I might also be able to fill in some of our questions. You go first."

"It appears as though their visitor left without taking her suitcase," said Collins. "There was enough clothing for at least a week. No license or other form of identification, but we took the clothes to the lab for a DNA sample. Whatever we get we can send to SLED to check for a match. I think we should know if she's the victim. Then all we have to do is locate the owners for her name."

"I'm not sure that'll be necessary," said Beulah Jean. "We actually have more information."

"Did you find someone in Seagrove who knows Bernice, the potter?"

"Up here she goes by Bonnie Kramer. Looks like she's the woman who stayed in that trailer. I was told she and her husband were having marital problems."

"Maybe that's why he didn't file a missing person's report," said Collins.

"I don't think that's why," said Beulah Jean. "Do you remember the wedding ring on the male victim?"

"Yeah. *Bonnie Forever 10-10-10*. Holy shit! He's her husband?"

"A real possibility. Jack and I are going to meet with the only police officer in this town as soon as we can find him. There's also a local brewery where Scout's been known to frequent. We'll check that out after we stop at the police station."

"I'm already looking through data bases for a Scout Kramer from Seagrove, North Carolina."

"The woman at the Pottery Museum tells me he's been having difficulty since he came back from Afghanistan," said Beulah Jean. "Maybe there's a military record on file. I can't believe his real name is Scout."

"I'd love to follow up right away. When are you planning to get back?"

"Jack and I have overnight reservations in Asheboro. I think we can check out the brewery tonight and go over to the Kramers' house and pottery shop tomorrow. We should be back by tomorrow night."

"Can you and Jack meet with my team on Thursday morning?"

"I'm not sure what Jack's schedule will allow, but I'll

be there."

"Thanks, Beulah Jean. I don't think we'd ever have gotten this far without you. See you Thursday."

Jack put Miss Shelby back in the car and walked around to the driver's seat.

Beulah Jean took her notes from the roof of the car and sat in the front seat.

"Should we head over to the police station?" she asked Jack. "We need to get into the Kramers' property. Unless they have someone staying there, we'll need to clear things with the authorities."

"Yeah. Why don't we try to find this Officer Griffin? I think there'll be more people at the brew house tonight after we check into our hotel. That way Miss Shelby can stretch out in a real room while we work instead of a back seat."

"You're right. Looks like the station is only two blocks east. Let's see if we can convince this guy to help us out. Otherwise, I can call Detective Collins and have him make all the arrangements for us."

"My money's on you, Babe. I've watched you operate. You could get a stop sign to change colors."

"You're setting my bar awfully high. What if I can't

convince him to let us in their place?

"Not even a possibility" said Jack starting the car for the ride to the station.

Laura Randolph was right. The police station door was locked. There was a note on the window explaining Officer Griffin was out of town. He left a phone number for calls other than the emergency number above in bold print.

"This must be his cell number," said Jack. "Not something I've ever made public."

"I think life around here calls for many changes in police work," said Beulah Jean. "Let's see if we can conjure up a response." She waited for someone to answer.

"Officer Griffin," said the rough voice.

Beulah Jean explained why she and Jack needed his help. He seemed pretty upset.

"You really think they're both dead?" he asked.

"It's a pretty real possibility," said Beulah Jean. "We'll need to find some DNA from their house or pottery shop to be sure."

"I have three part-time officers working with me. They usually cover the traffic issues. Not much happens in Seagrove. If I'm not back from Greensboro in the morning,

I'll get in touch with one of them and have you escorted to their house."

"Thanks for your help," said Beulah Jean. "Hope to see you in the morning."

They drove north for about twenty minutes before they saw the sign for the Hampton Inn in Asheboro. Jack took the bags from the car and headed for the registration desk, while Beulah Jean took Miss Shelby over to the wooded area on the side of the hotel to make sure she would be able to stay in the room while they went for dinner.

Across the street was a restaurant called Kickback Jacks, saving them the need to look any further. They sat at the bar and checked out the menu. Jack ordered the Ribs & Shrimp Combo and Beulah Jean decided on the Pan Seared Salmon.

"We'll have two Woodchuck Ambers," said Jack when asked what they wanted to drink.

"I'm still spinning from everything we uncovered today," said Beulah Jean. "Do you agree the dead man is Bonnie's husband?"

"Sure feels like he's the one they found in the mall. Maybe he went down there to find her."

"Do you think he could have killed her?" asked Beulah Jean.

"I think we need a lot more proof before we jump to that conclusion. But I'll admit it did cross my mind."

"I haven't been able to think about anything else since I made the connection. That inscription on his wedding ring can't be ignored."

They sat in silence watching the activity at the bar until their food arrived. Beulah Jean couldn't stop creating the rest of the Kramers' story in her head. Did Scout get clean and decide to find Bonnie? Did he find her at the campground? If so, maybe there's some evidence of him being in the trailer. Maybe he took his own life after realizing he couldn't live without her. What was the green sea glass doing in his hand? Was he using it to protect himself or to kill himself? Why was he shoeless?

Jack put his hand on Beulah Jean's arm, holding it steady. "A penny for your thoughts?" he said, wondering where her mind had wondered.

"Sorry. It will take at least a few hundred singles for

that information," she said bringing her thoughts back to dinner with Jack.

Chapter Twelve

They parked their car out back of the brewery and walked thru the darkened area of the building where the Four Saints Brewing Company operated their 7-barrel brewhouse. The noise level rose as soon as they opened the door to the actual pub. Beulah Jean and Jack found two empty seats at the bar and were given a flight of beer with their four choices from the latest offerings listed on the large chalkboard on the wall.

After tasting their picks, they settled on a pint of Bound to Get Down Pale Ale for Jack and an Upper Irish Red for Beulah Jean. The bartender brought them a complimentary pimento cheese and cracker plate.

"Are you new in town or just passing through?" asked the twenty-something male wearing the man bun and plaid shirt. He put a few napkins down in front of their snack.

"Actually, we're looking for a missing person," said

Beulah Jean handing him her card. "We were hoping someone might know Scout Kramer. We heard he came in here often."

"Scout is missing?"

"Yes. I assume you know him," said Jack. "When was the last time you saw him?"

"Well, I was off the last two weeks visiting my parents out west, but he was here when I closed the last night I worked."

Beulah Jean thought his answer couldn't be correct. "So, three weeks ago, he was in the area?"

"He spent most of the night right in the seat you're in. He was trying to make some life-changing decision. I just listened."

"So, he was a regular?" asked Jack.

"I used to be able to set my watch by him. He would arrive by seven and stay 'til closing. Then he went away for several weeks. Word was he dried out. When he came back, he only ordered our non-alcoholic spritzer."

"He was sober and still hung out at this place?" asked Jack.

"He wanted someone to talk to. His wife had left town,

and I think they were on the outs. He was very anxious to try to make things better. At least, he talked a lot about it. I assumed the reason I haven't seen him here this week was because he finally made the move to go get her."

"Did he say where he thought she was?" asked Beulah Jean.

"The beach was all he talked about."

"Did he say which beach?"

The bartender called out to a group of thirty-somethings sitting at a table closer to the windows upfront. "Seth, you know what beach Scout was talking about visiting?"

The man he called Seth got up from his table and walked over to the bar. He looked at Jack and said, "Who's asking?"

Jack had dealt with this kind of encounter on many occasions. He put out his hand for shaking. "I'm Detective Handy from South Carolina. Investigator Pickens and I are working a missing persons case. We were hoping to find someone who knows Scout Kramer."

"South Carolina, you say?"

"That's right," said Jack.

"We're from Myrtle Beah," said Beulah Jean handing

him her card. "Do you think Scout would have travelled there recently?"

"He's been gone a couple of weeks. Thought they'd be back by now. I'm getting worried about him. Why are you looking for him?"

"We're trying to identify a John Doe found dead in Myrtle Beach last week. Our information led us to Scout. We're trying to confirm what we've learned."

"Not Scout," said Seth in a choked voice. "I was his best man. We were in the service together. Got out two years ago, six days apart. He finally got through months of PTSD symptoms and was on the mend. He even thought Bonnie would be willing to give things a second chance. Are you sure he's dead?"

"No," said Beulah Jean. "That's why we're here. We need a DNA sample for testing, but we haven't gone out to his house yet. Officer Griffin is going to let us in tomorrow."

"Wasn't Bonnie able to identify him. She's in Myrtle Beach also. He went to find her."

"No. We haven't been able to find Bonnie," said Beulah Jean. She wasn't sure this former best man could handle hearing Bonnie might be the other dead body.

"Let me call his cell," said Seth. "This should settle any questions you have." He held his iPhone to his ear and waited for someone to answer. Nothing.

Beulah Jean noticed the fluid in Seth's eyes. He sniffled then spoke. "Hey Buddy, everyone's looking for you. Where the hell are you? Call me."

She could tell he was beginning to believe Scout was in real trouble. Maybe even dead.

"Listen," said Seth. "I'd like to go out to their place with you. Maybe I can find something that will help locate Scout. What time are you going?"

"We're hoping by ten tomorrow morning," said Beulah Jean, "But everything depends on when Officer Griffin can get us inside their house."

"Hell, I can get you inside. I know where they hide the spare key. Meet me here tomorrow morning and you can follow me out to their place."

"Great," said Jack. "We appreciate your help."

"This place doesn't open 'til four. I'll be parked out back in a black jeep."

"We'll find you," said Beulah Jean. "Thanks, again."

Seth walked back to his table and the conversation got

louder coming from that corner. Scout's name was heard over the noise. They all seemed concerned. This was one of those times when Beulah Jean found her job difficult.

Miss Shelby rested her head out the back window of Jack's car allowing the breeze to cool her face. They pulled up next to Seth's jeep in the brewery parking lot. Beulah Jean rolled down her window.

"I called Officer Griffin and told him you had a key and were taking us to the Kramer's," she told Seth. "I said I'd call him if there was any need to follow-up."

"We'll be there in fifteen or twenty minutes," said Seth. "After we turn off Alternate 220, the road follows a typical winding country trail. Just make sure you take the sharp left on to Jugtown Road. That dirt road will take us to the entrance of their property."

They saw at least twenty shops or galleries along Route 705, winding their way along a part of the country Beulah Jean had never seen. "Some of these places are calling me to stop and buy some of the pottery pictured on the signs directing me to their galleries."

"Nothing says we can't revisit this area before we head back to Myrtle Beach," said Jack.

"Nice thought, but right now my mind is only on one track. We need to find some DNA in order to identify Bonnie & Scout Kramer.

Jugtown Road wound left and the dirt road on the right led onto the Kramers' property. The sign in front of the long driveway said: *Pottery & Gem Heaven*. The road up the longer driveway on the left led toward a two-story brown-plank-house with green shutters. There was a brick patio out front with a green slatted swing on one side, and a small round wrought iron table and chairs on the other. As soon as they parked and got out of the car, Miss Shelby wandered over toward a narrow stream that wound around the back of the property.

"She'll be fine," she told Jack. "She's in her glory when she can roam like that. She'll stay close enough. Her radar won't let us leave without her."

Seth parked his jeep and went to the side of the house and came back with a key. "I'm not sure what we're going to find," said Seth. "Bonnie keeps a spotless house, but Scout was here last. His habits are NOT the same."

"You mean like most men," said Beulah Jean, trying to act like everything was not as critical as she was afraid to admit.

There was a pile of folded laundry on a chair in the kitchen, and a few dishes in the sink. Otherwise, the interior looked like people had not been there for a while. Dusty. A few plants in desperate need of water. A spider web running from the window over the sink to the café curtain keeping out the morning sun.

"What do you need for a DNA sample?" asked Seth.

"I guess are best chance would be a toothbrush or hairbrush," said Beulah Jean. "Anything that would have touched the person's body. We might find some DNA on that glass in the sink." She pulled out a baggie from her purse and put on a pair of gloves. Being careful not to wipe any leftover saliva from the glass, she put it in the bag and sealed it before placing it in the box Jack had taken from his car.

"Their bedroom is the one on the right at the top of the stairs," said Seth. "It's probably better if I don't touch any brush they might have left, so my prints don't complicate the test."

"Thanks," said Beulah Jean, taking the box from Jack. "You're right. I'll go up and see what I can find." When she got to the entrance of the Kramers' bedroom she stopped. The wedding picture was on the floor with a large crack running from the top to the bottom. The master bed was covered with women's clothing. Like they had been thrown on the bed in a fit of anger. Dresses, jeans, blouses and even a woman's bathrobe. She looked for a hamper that might have had some unwashed underwear. The master bath off the bedroom was clean but she did find a toothbrush in a lovely pottery holder on the vanity sink. She wasn't sure who it belonged to or how long it had been since someone used it. Everything fit in the box. Before she left the room, she took a picture with her iPhone of the wedding photo.

When she got back downstairs Jack was holding a piece of paper he found on the desk in the small room off to the left. She thought the space must have been used as an office. "This has Scout's real name. You might want to take a picture."

"Clyde Kramer?" said Beulah Jean.

"No one ever called him Clyde," said Seth. "After he met Bonnie, he never wanted anyone to call them Bonnie and Clyde. He thought it was a curse."

"Seth, do you think we could get into their pottery shop?" asked Beulah Jean.

"Yeah, the keys are on a hook in that office. I had to open up the shop for a customer once when they were both out of town."

They went outside and Miss Shelby was laying under the swing. "Told you she'd stay close," Beulah Jean said to Jack.

Seth locked the door to the house, and they followed him back down the dirt driveway to the cottage that held Bonnie's creations.

The pieces were lovely. Some almost magical. The colors of greens and blues with highlights of gold made for a wonderful display of work. Beulah Jean noticed an enclosed two-shelf glass counter display holding beautiful bracelets and earrings.

There was an entrance to what was once a large closet turned into her workshop in the back of the room. Beulah Jean looked around for something Bonnie used that might have been fresh enough for a DNA test. She bagged an old cloth on the side of the table obviously used for detail work.

Beulah Jean felt Bonnie's identification would not need DNA. The wedding picture still showed signs of the older woman found dead behind the Olive Shop at the mall. But any added confirmation would be appreciated by the Myrtle Beach Investigative Unit.

When she came back out into the room, she saw Jack and Seth talking in the corner. "What are you guys up to?" she asked.

Jack looked at Beulah Jean and held up some sea glass in his hand. "I noticed these in that box under the bookcase. Seth says Bonnie collected sea glass. She even made a few pieces of jewelry with it."

Beulah Jean took a breath. She walked over to the men and picked up a piece of sea glass. It was thicker than Brandy's offerings at Seaside Treasures. The green piece looked more like what Detectives Stone and Wexler found in the dead man's hand.

"Did Scout ever work with this sea glass?" she asked Seth.

"Hell, no. He never thought it was worth anything. He was a whittler."

"A what?" asked Jack. "You mean someone who carves

wood?"

"Yeah. He loved working on his carvings. Was like therapy to him once we came back from Afghanistan. There's a box of some of his stuff over here." He brought them to a small closet near the front door. When he opened the door, they could see several small carvings that were worth selling. "There's an area out here where he loved working." He opened a door and they walked out to a small porch with a table and chair in the corner. "I can still see him whittling and downing a brew sitting right in that chair," said Seth. "I can't believe he could be dead."

Beulah Jean ended up taking a couple pieces of sea glass and three small carvings of Scout's.

"Seth, we really appreciate your help with this mystery. I hope we are wrong about Scout."

"Will you call me when you are sure?" He handed Beulah Jean his card.

"As soon as I get the results," she assured him.

Jack carried the box and placed it into the trunk of his car. Miss Shelby rubbed her fur up against Seth's leg. She liked him. They said their goodbye's and got in their cars. Beulah Jean was afraid the next time she spoke with Seth the news would be bad.

Chapter Thirteen

"Jack got called back to the Isle of Palms for a new case," said Beulah Jean when she walked into Detective Collins' conference room. Detectives Stone and Wexler were already seated going over a report that came in from the lab.

"Sorry to hear that," said Doug Collins. "I was hoping to finally meet him. I heard good things about his work with you on the drug dealer case."

"He spends most weekends here in Market Common. I'm sure we can find a time to get you two together," said Beulah Jean.

She accepted a cup of coffee from Wexler and then took a seat across from him at the table. She put the box she carried from her car in the middle of the table and slid on a pair of gloves. As she pulled each item from the box, she explained where she found it and who she felt it belonged to before she placed the item on Wexler's tray.

He wrapped everything tightly and brought the package

out to an officer waiting to take it to the lab.

While he was out of the room, Stone informed Beulah Jean and Collins about the lab report he had received this morning.

"We did find a couple of toothbrushes in the trailer at the KOA Campground," said Stone. "We didn't know if they belonged to the owners or the dead woman. To be sure, we sent them to the lab. The suitcase we found had several items of clothing folded neatly inside. We assumed they had been washed since she wore them, but we took a couple anyway. There weren't any dirty dishes in the sink. The woman kept the place pretty clean. We did find a napkin in the trash we assumed she used before leaving the trailer. That might be the only item with a DNA sample we could use."

"Did you call SLED for the DNA lab results they have in custody?" asked Collins.

"Called them yesterday," said Stone. "We're expecting the information from SLED this afternoon by courier. The results from the napkin will be on the report. We're hoping there's a match."

"Good," said Collins. "You can bring it over to our lab

when it arrives."

"That might not be necessary," said Beulah Jean. She took out her iPhone and showed them the wedding picture she took at the Kramers' house. "I think you can see the resemblance to our dead woman," she said.

"Like a risen ghost," said Wexler walking behind Beulah Jean when he returned to the conference room. "That's definitely the woman they have at SLED.

"I believe the man in the picture is your dead man," she said. "His name is Scout. They were married and having problems."

"Well, we finally solved one murder," said Collins.

"I don't think so," said Beulah Jean. "Jack and I spoke with the bartender at the brewery last night. He's positive Scout was in his bar three weeks ago. That would have been after she was murdered."

"He could have murdered her and gone back to Seagrove," said Collins. "You can't rule that out."

"I guess it's a possibility. But the bartender said he came in every night and was talking about coming to the beach to find his wife. I don't think he killed her."

The Myrtle Beach Investigative Unit was not buying her story. She knew they believed Scout murdered his wife. Beulah Jean pulled a bag out of her tote and laid it on the table.

"These samples were in Bonnie's pottery shop," she said pulling the green sea glass from the bag and laying it on a sterile pad on the table.

"That looks exactly like the piece held in our dead man's hand when we found him," said Wexler. "What a twist. There's no way she could have murdered him. She was already dead."

Beulah Jean pulled the whittled carvings out of her bag. "These were also found in a place where Scout worked according to his best friend. There were at least two dozen completed pieces."

"So, the man was a whittler, said Stone. "Did you find any knives he used to make these?"

Beulah Jean pulled out a wrapped oblong object. She took off the paper and showed them two knives. "There were several different sizes like these in the room. I thought you might be able to get some DNA from them."

"This roller coaster doesn't stop. I'm feeling dizzy."

said Stone before taking the knives out to the other room to prepare them for testing.

"I'm not sure any of the whittled pieces or the tools used to make them with will prove to be useful," said Beulah Jean. "I just couldn't ignore them."

"In fact, I'm not sure we need to test anything I brought here today," she said.

"We could just ask Seth, Scout's friend, to come in and identify the body. I didn't have that authority, or I would have asked myself."

"You're right," said Collins. "We can do that. However, now that we have all this, let's wait for the results. If they don't prove solid, I will get that contact information from you and bring him in."

"Even if we identify the dead man, we still don't have the murderer, said Beulah Jean. "For either body."

"Certainly not for the man you're calling Scout Kramer," said Collins. "I'm not convinced he didn't murder his wife."

Beulah Jean could see she was not going to convince them until they found solid evidence proving Scout was not in the area when his wife was murdered. She had other questions for the crime scene unit.

"Have you found out anything new about Dan Logan from the Kitchen Cutlery Shop?

"We have him staying at a hotel in Houston," said Wexler. "The only place he seems to go from there is to the cancer facility at MD Anderson. He may be visiting a sick relative. We're trying to verify why he's there, and whether he still has a connection to the woman's murder."

"So do you still think he could have murdered Bonnie Kramer?"

"We're not ready to drop him from our persons of interest list," said Stone. "Especially after the knives you discovered in Seagrove. The knives you brought here look a lot like the ones we've seen in his shop. There could be a connection."

"You think there's a connection between Dan Logan and Scout Kramer?" said Beulah Jean. "Like maybe he killed Bonnie for Scout? I suppose we won't know for sure without further proof."

"Did you locate any relatives of the Kramer's while you were in Seagrove?" asked Detective Collins. "I suppose we need to notify her family. That picture is enough for me, but it won't hurt to wait another twenty-four hours when we have solid DNA evidence."

"According to Seth, they had no siblings, and their parents are dead," said Beulah Jean. "I think the aunt who owns that trailer at the KOA Campgrounds would be the next of kin."

"We still haven't had any contact with the owners," said Collins. "Our search of the trailer was supervised by the manager at the campground. She had to observe according to their policy because we showed up with the search warrant. She told us nobody in the long-term area had reached the Harrisons."

"Wow," said Beulah Jean. "Some people know how to vacation in peace. I'm not sure being that invisible is practical. I was told they went to visit their daughter who had just delivered a baby. You'd think someone at the campground would have been given contact information in case of an emergency."

"We'll keep on it," said Collins. "I'm more concerned about what we tell them about how she died. If you are that convinced her husband didn't do the deed, we have a lot of stones to overturn before we can settle this case."

"I think the sea glass I found in Seagrove is the most disturbing to me," said Beulah Jean. "I can't figure out if Scout took some from Bonnie's shop or was taking a piece he found here in Myrtle Beach back to Seagrove."

"I suppose either theory could be correct," said Collins. "I'm not even sure how we're going to find out."

"I kept a few pieces in my car," said Beulah Jean. "I plan to bring them to Brandy at Seaside Treasures in the mall. I'd like to get her take on where they might have been found or anything else she knows about them."

"Be careful," said Collins. "We have her on our list for a reason. Now she has moved closer to the top. With the piece we found in the dead man's hand, she could move from a person of interest to a real suspect."

Beulah Jean knew she was taking a chance by letting the detectives know about the sea glass. She was playing with fire. But she was convinced Brandy wasn't involved with either case. In fact, her expertise was what she counted on for the next step of her investigation.

"Please let me know when the DNA results arrive. I have some messages that need my attention."

"Thank you, Beulah Jean," said Collins. "What you've

uncovered is invaluable to our team. We will let you know as soon as we hear from the lab."

Getting over to the mall was on the top of her list. She phoned Brandy from her car on her way there. Brandy was sitting behind the counter when Beulah Jean entered the shop. She walked over to the counter and placed her tote on top. When she pulled out the sea glass, Brandy stood and leaned closer.

"Where did you find these?" she asked.

"At the dead woman's pottery shop," said Beulah Jean.

"Wait. I thought it was the man who had a piece of sea glass in his hand. Not the woman."

"You're correct."

"I don't get it."

"I'm hoping you can help me figure things out. Do you have any idea where these pieces might have been found?"

"The Brunswick Islands in North Carolina have been very good places to find sea glass. Ocean Isle Beach, about an hour before the tide goes out, has proved bountiful. The tourists find more sea glass on North Myrtle Beach than the beaches further south."

"Are these pieces typical of the sea glass found north of

here?" asked Beulah Jean.

"I'm not ruling out the possibility of finding these in Myrtle Beach, but if I wanted to be sure to come home with something worth placing in a piece of jewelry or on a piece of art, I'd go north."

"Would you say these fall in the category of the pieces you buy from your dealer or ones found on the local beaches?"

"These are definitely more common," said Brandy. "I wouldn't use them in my work."

Beulah Jean had seen a piece of jewelry in Bonnie's shop that looked like this common glass was used. Most of her pottery was leaning on the earthy side. Not sure Bonnie would buy the better grade pieces for her art.

"Thanks, Brandy. I'm not convinced the dead woman didn't use the Myrtle Beach glass in her jewelry. I'll hold on to these a little longer."

She left Brandy's and decided to walk by the Kitchen Cutlery shop to see if Daniel Logan had returned. She could tell from the end of the aisle there were no lights in his store. She walked up to the front window and noticed something on the back shelf for the first time. An entire row of whittled angels. How had she missed those until now?

Chapter Fourteen

Beulah Jean took out her iPhone and snapped a picture through the store window of the whittled angels. She decided to keep this information to herself. Before she could put the phone back in her purse, Margie Kane appeared next to her.

"I thought I saw you leaving Seaside Treasures," said Margie.

"You did, indeed," said Beulah Jean.

"I planned to call you today. I have some information you might find helpful."

Beulah Jean knew Margie had a reputation for gossip, but sometimes people who are prone to looking for answers actually come up with workable theories.

"I'm all ears," said Beulah Jean.

"Well. I came in early yesterday and saw there were lights on in this shop. Of course, I thought there might be news about Mr. Logan. So, I knocked on the window and a young woman opened the door. Turns out she's his sister."

"Dan Logan's sister?"

"Yes. I asked her if she knew when Dan would be returning. I guess no one else had contacted her. I'm surprised the management wasn't all over this situation like bees in a honey jar," said Margie.

Beulah Jean agreed. She was planning to contact the management for any information they could share about Dan's return, figuring they must be concerned about leaving a store closed for this long. Surely, they could rent it to another merchant.

"What did his sister have to say?" asked Beulah Jean.

"She said Dan is in treatment for cancer. He thought he was just going for a follow-up exam. When they took the scan, they found a tumor that needed immediate attention. He'll be there for at least six weeks of treatment."

"I'm sorry to hear that," said Beulah Jean. "Did she tell you she was closing the shop?"

"No. She said Dan had a supplier who would be taking over the shop. Someone he's been dealing with for at least six months. According to Dan's sister, his supplier has been trying to convince Dan to retire for months. He's happy to be able to run the store."

"Do you know what merchandise the supplier sold to Dan?" asked Beulah Jean.

"All she knew was that he was a craftsman," said Margie.

Beulah Jean was surprised to hear a supplier of the knives wasn't taking over. There were very few handmade items in the shop.

"When do you think the transition will take place?"

"Right away. I think he lives in the Myrtle Beach area. Sounds like things will open by this weekend. Dan's sister flew back to Houston last night."

"Thanks for the information, Margie. Please let me know when you see the shop is open."

Beulah Jean was anxious to speak to the craftsman who will be running the shop. Maybe she could finally clear Dan's name from the person of interest list. Right now, she needed to drive over to the KOA Campground and speak to the woman who gave her the information about Bonnie – who is also known as Bernice.

She was hoping to hear some good news about the Harrisons who owned the trailer. As Bonnie's only known relatives, they needed to hear the truth. By the end of the day, Detective Collins should have the proof he needs to declare her identification and notify her next of kin.

She found the woman sitting on the swing with her knitting needles moving her yarn into the afghan on her lap – at least a foot longer than the last time she visited.

"Hello, Mrs. Clarkson. How are you today?" said Beulah Jean. "Have the Harrisons returned from visiting their daughter?"

"Everyone is asking," said Dorothy Clarkson. "We've even had the police here three times. What do you think they're looking for? I hope nothing happened to the Harrisons or their daughter."

"I think it's about Bernice. The young woman you spoke with when she visited last month."

"I haven't seen her either," said Dorothy. "My guess is that she went back to her husband. I got the impression she was leaning in that direction. I really liked Bernice. I was planning to ask the Harrisons for her address. I want to send her a greeting card to let her know I'm thinking about her."

"That's very kind of you," said Beulah Jean. "I'm sure

she would appreciate your concern." She didn't have the heart to tell Dorothy what she knew. She needed to leave. Soon enough the news would become public.

As she was walking away, she remembered the reason she came. "Dorothy, did Bernice ever mention looking for sea glass on the beach?"

"She did. Showed me a pretty handful one afternoon. Said she used some in her sterling bracelets and even showed me a picture of a vase she made with sea glass accents."

"Did she tell you wear she found it?"

"I think right down here at the inlet on the beach around sixth street. I know that was her favorite spot for sunning. She even sat there and listened to the country singers at the festival."

"Thanks, Dorothy. You've been very helpful once again. Good luck finishing that afghan." Beulah Jean couldn't wait to head for the beach.

There were several groups of sunbathers gathered near the Sixth-Street inlet. Beulah Jean took off her shoes and rolled up her pants as soon as she crossed over a section of sea oats. Walking slowly by the first group of bikini-clad twenty-somethings, she heard enough of their conversation to determine they were on vacation and hadn't been in Myrtle Beach long enough to have seen Bonnie Kramer.

About fifty feet south, she saw a couple of seniors sitting under an umbrella. By the time she got close enough to speak to them, she overheard them arguing over leaving for an early bird offering nearby.

"Hi," she said as she walked closer. "Do you come here often?"

"About four or five times a week," said the sixty-something woman brushing sand off her feet and pulling her clogs out of her beach bag. "Only after three when the sun isn't as strong. You know, skin cancer and all."

"I was hoping you might have seen a woman in her thirties around here a few weeks ago. I'm told she liked this area and would look for sea glass."

"You mean Bernice?" asked the woman.

Beulah Jean caught herself with her right foot as she started to fall over when she heard the woman's response.

"Yes. Her name was Bernice. Did you know her?"

"Some of us knew her better than others," said the man

as he got up out of his beach chair.

"Louie, stop it," said the woman.

"Well. It's true."

"I think you're jealous you aren't single and able to date."

Beulah Jean knew there was a story there she needed to hear. "Did Bernice have admirers who visited this section of beach?"

"You could say that I suppose," said Louie. He folded his chair and took down the umbrella. "At least one."

"Louie," said the woman. "We don't know anything about him at all." She folded the towel she pulled from the back of her chair. "He could have been her father."

"You think she might have been here with an older man?" asked Beulah Jean.

"Louie's imagination takes over sometimes," said the woman. "Bernice came to the beach by herself almost every day for nearly a month. Then one day this older man came by. He walked up from the water and started talking with her and the next thing we knew he was sitting down."

Louie leaned in closer to Beulah Jean. "The rest is history. He came with her every day after that – until they both disappeared."

"Did you ever speak with Bernice before the man started coming?"

"She was very sad," said the woman. "We knew she was talking about going back to her husband who had PTSD issues."

"Do you think the man who started coming with her was her husband?"

"Never," said Louie. "He was definitely on the make. Nearly mauled her."

"Louie!" yelled the woman. "That's enough. We don't know anything of the sort. You're jealous."

"Don't take my word for it," said Louie. "Ask the bartender at Clamdiggers Pub on Ocean Boulevard. We saw them in there several times."

"We go there for the early bird specials. There's a lot of regulars who come in for their clam special."

"So, Bernice never told you about her male visitor? asked Beulah Jean.

"She used to talk to us almost every day, mostly about the sea glass she found," said the woman. "After he arrived, we never spoke to her again. I'm not even sure if she's still in the area."

"Did you ever see him looking for sea glass with her?"

"Only the first day he appeared," said Louie. "After that he wanted all her attention. No time for distractions."

"Come on, Louie. I've heard enough. That imagination of yours is working overtime. Besides, I'm getting hungry."

"Thanks for the information," said Beulah Jean. "Enjoy your dinner."

She walked back over the dunes and rolled down her pant legs and put on her shoes. Now she had to find the Clamdigger Pub.

Chapter Fifteen

Beulah Jean adjusted her eyes after she entered the pub. Coming from the bright sunlight was a shock to her pupils. When she took a seat at the bar, the bartender looked up from unloading clean glasses from the dishwasher.

"What can I get you?" he asked. "Everything's on happy hour prices right now."

"I'll have a glass of your house Pino Grigio." She pulled a folded paper menu from between the salt and pepper shakers on the bar.

He placed the glass of wine in front of Beulah Jean and noticed she was looking at the menu. "Are you interested in one of our early bird specials?"

"They do look inviting, but right now I'm interested in asking you a few questions," she said handing him her business card.

He placed the card in the back pocket of his jeans and continued unloading glasses from the dishwasher. She could tell he wasn't comfortable talking about customers.

Especially not to private investigators. Bartenders hear tales of bad relationships on a regular basis. It's part of the job. Most times they aren't even listening.

"I'm trying to find out if you've ever seen this woman," she asked showing him the picture of Bonnie she took out of her bag.

"Yeah. I remember her. She came in with an older guy almost every day for about two or three weeks. Then nothing. I figured she went back home."

"So, you don't think they lived together? You say she was with an older man. What fifty, sixty?"

"Yeah, maybe late fifties, early sixties. He looked even older. Or maybe she just looked a lot younger."

A thirty-something male in a three-piece suit came in and sat two stools away from Beulah Jean. He was obviously there for the happy hour drinks. He ordered a Bud Light and asked the bartender for a bowl of peanuts.

"How's sales today?" asked the bartender when he placed the nuts on the counter.

"Slow day. Not much call for new cars we can't get into the showroom for six months."

"Hey, you remember that couple who came in almost

every day and sat in that corner?" the bartender asked the man in the suit while pointing across the bar.

"You mean the May – December couple? Haven't seen them lately."

Beulah Jean knew he was referring to their age. More people used that phrase when the woman was the older member of the couple. But she was clear about what he meant. The man Bonnie was with was definitely not her husband. She needed more information.

"You were indicating that you didn't think they were living together?" she asked the bartender wanting to continue her query. "What gave you that idea?"

"For starters," the bartender began, "they didn't always leave together. And, towards the end of the time they came here they seemed to be fighting a lot. In the beginning he was all over her. Kissing her neck and rubbing her thigh."

"Like maybe they had just met?" asked Beulah Jean.

"A hundred percent," said the man in the suit. "He was on the make. Always suggesting she go with him to his place. It was obvious."

"Did he say where his place was?"

"One of those new upscale apartment complexes near

the mall," said the bartender. "He showed her a brochure one day touting all the amenities. She left it on the bar when they left."

"So maybe she finally agreed, and they are living happily together in his place," said Beulah Jean.

"I wouldn't put money on it," said the bartender. "The last time they were in she had a few too many and their conversation got loud. She talked about going back home. And she meant without him. He got pretty angry. After a few more drinks, she could hardly stand. He nearly carried her out of here. I haven't seen them since."

"How long ago would you say that happened?"

"Probably more than a month. Yeah, it was right after the crowd from the country western music festival left town."

"Thanks. You've been very helpful," said Beulah Jean. She paid for her wine and left the pub.

Instead of driving back to her place, she decided to see if Detective Collins was still in his office. His door was open when she arrived.

"Well, if it isn't my most productive non-employee," said Collins.

"I was hoping Stone and Wexler would still be in the building. I need to unload a mound of information. I thought maybe some of it would match their findings."

"They just left for the mall. The new guy running the Kitchen Cutlery is supposed to be there."

She brought him up to date with the information about the older man who she thought should be a person of interest in Bonnie's death.

"I suppose you didn't get a name on that older guy?"

"No, but I got an address – or at least a place he might call home. I'm planning to visit the complex tomorrow. If I can narrow it down to a real name, I'll get back to you. Let me know what your guys find out about the new Kitchen Cutlery manager. Something about the entire situation has the hairs on my arms dancing."

She still wasn't ready to mention the whittled angels on the store shelf. After seeing the display in Bonnie's shop at Seagrove, she was sure there was some kind of connection. She just couldn't be sure what form that would take.

When she pulled into her driveway out back of her townhouse, Jack's car was parked in her usual spot. He was sitting on her swing under the oak tree reading a magazine.

Miss Shelby was sleeping under the swing.

"Hey, I didn't realize you were coming north today," she said putting up her canvas top on her convertible. "Anything wrong?"

His smile confirmed her need to see him more often. "Should I have called you first?" he asked. "I thought when you gave me a key, we lost some of the need for formality."

"Absolutely. You are welcome here anytime. I'm pleasantly surprised. If I knew you were coming, I would have picked up some steaks on my way home."

"Not a problem. I'm craving Italian. Let's go back over to Maggi Ds. I have something I want to talk to you about."

Beulah Jean took her notebook she had been using in Detective Collins' office from her passenger seat and placed it in her bag with the rest of the notes she had taken from her meeting with the couple on the beach and the ones from the Clamdigger Bar. She walked over to the swing, dropped her bag, and sat down next to Jack. "What'cha got here?" she said looking at the magazine he was holding.

Miss Shelby got up and came over to Beulah Jean. She rubbed her face along Beulah Jean's leg. The two had been together a long time. A simple face massage was mora than appreciated by the golden retriever.

"Hey you two. I want in," said Jack as he placed his arm around Beulah Jean and kissed her hard and long.

"Okay. Got the message. Let me get Miss Shelby her dinner and then we can head over to Maggi Ds. What do you want to talk to me about?"

Jack closed his magazine and got up off the swing. "Not now. Let's have a few drinks first. You're parked behind me. Mind if we go in your car?"

The bar at Maggi Ds was nearly full, but they found two empty seats at the end by the Italian Cookie display. Before they were seated, they heard John ask, "A Yuengling draft and a Pino Grigio?"

They stopped half-seated. "Boy this guy is good," said Jack. "You read our minds," even though he hadn't given any thought to what he wanted.

John placed their drinks in front of them along with menus and said, "Cynthia will be right with you," as she came out from the kitchen and walked up behind him.

"You guys should take this show on the road," said Jack.

"Are you hungry or do you want to wait awhile?" asked Cynthia folding open a new page in the notebook where she placed all her orders.

"We're in no hurry and have a lot to discuss," said Jack.

"No problem. Flag me down when you're ready."

Beulah Jean waited until Cynthia left the bar. "What's all this about - 'a lot to discuss?'" she asked.

He pulled a magazine out from his back pocket. He had stuck it there when he got up from the swing. Opening it to the section he had marked with a folded page, he asked, "Have you ever been to Nantucket Island?"

"Never. I've always thought of it as a place for the elite. You know the Kennedys, Oprah Winfrey, Kirk Douglas, Bruce Willis. Lots of celebrities. That picture looks amazing. Where is that?"

"It's the White Elephant Resort near downtown Nantucket, not far from the ferry landing." He turned the page and there were several other Nantucket highlights decorated for the holidays.

"I thought we might enjoy spending Thanksgiving in one of these beauties. What do you think?"

Beulah Jean took a moment. She hadn't planned a trip

like this since Adam died. They had gone to several island hot spots while waiting for him to get his divorce. Mostly in the Caribbean or Mexico – never any place north of Atlanta. This would be the first time she and Jack would go away for fun and relaxation – not their short trips for work.

"Sounds wonderful," she said. "Do you think we could actually pull it off, with your schedule and my latest investigations?

"We can if you say yes, and I get started with the arrangements. We can work around your latest cases, and I told you how much time I've accumulated waiting for someone to travel with. Besides, aren't you getting close to clearing your clients' names?"

"Even if I find Bonnie's killer, there's still the problem of her husband, Scout. My clients won't be removed from the suspect list until both cases are solved."

She pulled out her phone and searched for a picture. "I think I might be on to a new suspect. Look at these whittled angels I spotted on a shelf in the Kitchen Cutlery shop."

"They look just like the ones Scout had in his work area in Bonnie's North Carolina shop," said Jack. "Did you ask who made them?"

"I haven't had a chance. There hasn't been anyone in there since Dan left for Texas. However, a new guy is supposed to be running the place starting this week. In fact, Wexler and Stone should be over there as we speak to see what they can find out about my client."

"This could all come together soon," said Jack. "I'll drink to that possibility." He got Cynthia's attention.

"More drinks or are you ready for dinner?" she asked.

"Both," said Jack.

"I'll have your Veal Parm. What about you, Hon?" he said putting his arm around her shoulder.

Beulah Jean pushed her phone over to the side to check out the specials on the menu.

"Did you buy one of his angels?" asked Cynthia looking at the picture on the phone.

Beulah Jean felt the hairs on the back of her neck standing up. She looked at Cynthia with confusion. "Do you know the guy who makes these?" she asked.

"Well. I know a guy who whittles angels. I saw one he brought into the restaurant one time to give to a customer. Not sure if they're the ones in your picture."

"What's the guy's name?"

"Haven't a clue. He comes in here once in a while. We call him Joe. Always pays cash, so I never see a name on a credit card. We use Joe when we have a returning customer whose name we don't know. It's better than John Doe." She looked over to the other end of the bar. "Hey John, you remember the guy with the whittled angels?"

"How can I forget," said John. "He always leaves little piles of saw dust on my bar stools or floor. I think he has wood shavings in the pockets of everything he wears."

Beulah Jean asked the question she thought she knew the answer to, "Do you know where he lives?"

"I think he lives down the street in those new luxury apartments," said Cynthia.

Beulah Jean ordered the Chicken Marsala, but after only two or three bites asked if she could get a box to take it home. She needed to call Detective Collins and makes plans to spend tomorrow at the apartments.

Chapter Sixteen

Beulah Jean arrived at Sovana, the new luxury apartment complex, and waited in the parking lot for Detective Stone. When she called Detective Collins, he was more than willing to assign Stone to work with her in case she was right about the possibility that Bonnie's killer might be a resident of Sovana.

His unmarked car pulled up next to her and the forty-year-old detective smiled when he saw her. Alex Stone could pass for a model in a GQ Magazine. In his navy-blue suit, he looked like an executive ready to move into the luxury apartments.

They walked into the lobby and a thirty-something blonde woman behind a marble counter welcomed them like they would be her next commission.

"Can I get you a Perrier or a non-alcoholic energy drink?" she asked as she pulled a folder from under the desk.

It was a marketing package about Sovana.

"No thank you," said Beulah Jean. "I'm Investigator Pickens and this is Detective Stone. We're looking for a person of interest we think might be a resident. Wondering if we could talk somewhere private?"

They each showed her their identification.

"Yes," she said. "I'm Sheila. Please come into my office."

They moved across the hall and sat in leather seats at a round glass table in the corner of the room. Beulah Jean pulled some notes and a pen from her bag and started the conversation.

"I believe the man we're looking for would be in his late fifties or early sixties."

"You're talking about more than half of our resident population," said Sheila.

"This man might have a hobby. We think he whittles statues."

"I think you're referring to Mr. Maxwell. We call him Max. He moved in about two months ago. I think he sells some of his crafts over at the mall."

"What is Mr. Maxwell's first name?" asked Stone.

"It's Howard. Howard Maxwell."

"Do you know if he's here now?" asked Beulah Jean. "We'd like to have a word with him.

"As a matter of fact, he's not. He left on vacation. He had a visitor last week and I think he went to the west coast with him. At least some of the residents overheard a conversation about his trip."

"This friend," said Beulah Jean. "Could you describe him?"

"I think I can do better than that. We had a pool party when he was here. I took a lot of pictures for our new brochure." She got up and went to her desk. She took out a folder filled with pictures of the resort. Some with residents enjoying many of the amenities. She chose two pictures and handed them to Beulah Jean. "This is Max," she said pointing to a man in excellent shape wearing a bathing suit. "His visitor was here then. That's him standing next to Max."

"Looks like they both work out," said Stone.

"They did spend a lot of time in our gym," said Sheila.

"I'm afraid we're going to have to ask you to let us see his apartment," said Beulah Jean.

"Oh, I can't do that. We have a very strict policy about privacy. I've probably broken it already by giving you all the information I just shared."

"I think this will keep you out of trouble," said Stone, showing her a search warrant. He had one prepared asking to search the apartment of their person of interest leaving the space for a name blank. No specific individual. He filled in the name.

"I'll need to call my social director from her activity to man the desk. Please wait for me in the library," she said pointing to a room across the lobby.

When she returned, she led them to the elevator which took them to the third floor. The hardwood floors along the hall gave them the feeling of walking on a cushion. Sheila took them to the corner unit. This was one of the more expensive apartments in the building. The room was dark even though there were windows on two walls. The blinds were pulled closed masking the view to the balcony as were the ones on the window overlooking the pool.

Both Beulah Jean and Detective Stone pulled on their gloves and began opening doors in the entertainment unit and end tables in the living room. They were empty.

When they walked into the master bedroom, Beulah Jean confirmed what she feared. Max was not coming back. The closet had nothing hanging, but there was a bag on the floor. It contained some wood shavings, a knife, and a number of green plastic garbage bags crumbled in a ball. Stone began taking pictures and then called Detective Collins to ask for the Crime Scene Unit.

Sheila was acting like a nervous cat. "I'm going to need to call my boss," she said walking back and forth from one end of the room to the other.

"I'll need a copy of that picture of Max with his visitor," said Beulah Jean. "Is there anyone in the building who would have spoken with Max about his friend or his trip?"

"There were several residents in attendance at the party. Max was very friendly. Sold a lot of his whittled works to neighbors. I think the neighbor across the hall from Max sat with him often during happy hour. He might know more."

Beulah Jean needed as much information as she could gather before she left the building. She went across the hall and knocked. The neighbor opened the door after the first knock. She thought he must have been listening to the activity in Max's apartment.

"Hi," said Beulah Jean. "I'm investigating a case here in Myrtle Beach that might prove Howard Maxwell a person of interest. I understand you were friendly with him." She found herself having trouble looking away from his long curly mustache. It clearly stood out at least an inch on each side of his face. She wondered if it was held that way with hairspray.

"I'd say Howard was friendly with a lot of the residents here at Sovana. But yes, I did spend some time with him over drinks during our regular happy hours."

"Did he mention going away on vacation?"

"No. I was surprised to see his newspapers piled up by the door the other day. I picked them up and brought them into my place. Figured I'd give them to him when he returned."

"So, there's no reason for you to think he might not return?" asked Beulah Jean.

"Of course not. Not now especially. He just got a deal he's been working on for weeks. He's going to be running his own shop in the mall. Why would you think he wouldn't return?"

"All his clothes and much of his personal belongings seem to be gone from his apartment. Did you meet his recent visitor? I believe Sheila said they worked out a lot during his visit. What can you tell me about him?"

"Well, he's from Venice Beach in California. He was staying at the Hilton Garden Inn over on the other side of the mall. But he spent more time here than at the hotel. "I can't say as I know him well. We played poker one night here at Sovana. He talked about moving in here. I believed he was close to putting down the required deposits. We even had dinner one night over at Maggi Ds."

"So, Max and his visitor were good friends?"

"They seemed to have a past together. Don't know exactly how or why, but they could read each other's mind. Had a lot of inside jokes. Like maybe they were in the service together."

"Did you get his name?" asked Beulah Jean.

"You know…I never did. Max called him Bro. Kind of endearing. They weren't really brothers. He just called him Bro like you would a close friend. I never questioned Max about his relationship with his friend."

Detective Stone walked over to Beulah Jean.

"The Crime Scene Unit is downstairs. I'm going to bring them up. I'm done here. I got a call from Detective Collins about an abandoned car over at Hilton Garden Inn. Seems like every time I'm in the middle of a case, I get called out on another."

"Wait, Alex," said Beulah Jean. "There may be a connection to our case. Max's neighbor here tells me the friend who visited Max was staying at the Hilton Garden Inn. I'm coming with you. And ask one of the Crime Scene Unit members to come as well. I think we need to get prints and anything else we might find."

She pulled one of her cards from her pocket and handed it to Max's neighbor.

"If you remember anything else about Max's visitor, please give me a call."

Beulah Jean and Alex thanked Sheila for her cooperation and said they were bringing in the Crime Scene Unit to take over. Both were sure they were in the apartment of Bonnie's killer.

Beulah Jean's phone rang as she was driving her car to the Hilton Garden Inn. She pulled into the hotel's parking lot and took the call.

"I hear you hit paydirt," said Collins at the other end of the line. "You keep rising on my list of detectives I want to try to persuade to join my crew."

"You can keep trying, but I'm quite happy handling things on my own," she said.

"Listen," said Collins, "I just got a call from Mrs. Harrington from the KOA Campground. She's back in town after spending a month with her daughter and the new granddaughter. She went this morning and identified Bonnie's belongings. We told her about Scout. She's not in a good place right now. Do you think you could stop by her trailer? Maybe she could give us a lead on his killer."

"Not a problem," said Beulah Jean. "I'm over here at the Hilton Garden Inn with Stone. I have a feeling this abandoned car could be Scout's. As soon as we're through here, I'll head over to the campground.

"Hard to believe we could be closing in on our killer. What luck."

"Don't put a period on the end of that sentence yet," said Beulah Jean. "I'll keep you posted."

Chapter Seventeen

Beulah Jean and Stone pulled into the Hilton Garden Inn in separate cars. Stone went over to a car in the back of the a with a large red sticker on the front window. He called in the plates and found out it belonged to Clyde Kramer of North Carolina. The member of the crime scene investigative unit who rode over from the Sovana apartments with him used her special tool to open the car door. She immediately went to work tagging items in the back seat of Scout's car before lifting prints.

Beulah Jean needed to find the manager on duty. She walked into the lobby and spoke to the clerk at the front desk.

"I'm Investigator Pickens," she said handing the woman her card. "We're responding to your call about the abandoned car in your parking lot. It appears to belong to the man found dead in the mall two weeks ago." She showed the clerk a copy of the picture of Scout and Bonnie from their bedroom dresser. "Do you recognize this man?"

"Yes. He was here for nearly two weeks. Quiet guy. Sat at our bar a few times. I kind of felt bad for him. Seemed lonely."

"Was he always alone?"

"Anytime I saw him, he was. But there is an incident report on file about a fight he had the last night he stayed with us. I wasn't here, but our late-night clerk said it got pretty rowdy near closing. He was ready to call the police, but they took it outside and left the premises."

"And you never saw him after that night?"

"No. I didn't see him the next morning. He used our automatic check-out system. He never came to the desk. Left his key cards in his room."

Beulah Jean looked for the picture of Max and his friend from the apartments. She showed the clerk. "Do you recognize either of these men?"

"That man was a guest of ours," she said pointing to Max's friend from Venice, California. "I'm not sure about the other. He does look familiar, but I don't think he stayed with us."

"I'll need his name and address," said Beulah Jean. "When does the night clerk come on duty? I want to talk with him."

"Lefty comes in at four. We overlap during check-in hours. He stays until midnight when our bar closes."

Stone came in from the parking lot. He was on the phone with Detective Collins. "Did Kramer stay here?" he asked when he got off the phone. "We got a positive on his car. They're sending a tow truck to bring it over to our lot as soon as the crime scene crew has finished here."

"Yes," said Beulah Jean. "He was a guest here for several nights according to the clerk. She's gone into her office for the exact dates. She's also sure this guy was here at the same time," she said pointing to Max's friend.

"So, the three of them could have been responsible for the wife's death."

"I'm not sure," said Beulah Jean. "There was some kind of altercation the night before Scout's death. Maybe Scout found out what they did and was going to turn the other two in for murder. I'm going to come back later when the night clerk comes on duty. He was a witness to the incident. His information could be vital to our case."

Stone's phone rang. He walked away and took the call. When he returned his face gave away his latest bit of information. "You're not going to believe this," he said putting both hands in the air like a member of a church congregation yelling *Alleluia*. "The crime scene unit found a pair of women's shoes under Max's bed. I asked them to text me a picture. Here it is now."

"I knew it," said Beulah Jean.

The clerk came out from the back office with paperwork. "It appears as though Mr. Kramer stayed with us for six nights," she said handing the invoice over to Beulah Jean.

"This confirms the day he checked out was the morning we found him inside the mall," said Beulah Jean showing the paperwork to Stone.

"I've got to get over to our impound lot with Kramer's car," said Stone. "There's a lot of paperwork necessary to release it to the next of kin."

"Speaking of next of kin. I'm going over to the Harrisons at the KOA Campground. Text me that picture. I want her to identify those shoes the crime scene found under Max's bed."

"And what about the other man in the picture," she asked the clerk. Do you have the dates of his stay?"

"I'm not sure of the identity of that man. Our night clerk will probably be able to identify him."

"Fine," said Beulah Jean. "I have an appointment. I'll be back at four."

"I'll meet you back here around four." Said Stone. "We can interview the night clerk together."

On the drive over to the campground Beulah Jean called Jack. "Can you believe Cynthia from Maggi D's broke my case wide open?" she asked Jack.

"You mean the whittler she said lived in the nearby apartments is your killer?"

"If not the killer, he certainly appears to be an accomplice."

"I think we'll have to increase her tip next time."

"At least," said Beulah Jean. "I spent the morning in his apartment. However, it looks like he's disappeared. Closets and drawers are empty. Although they did find a pair of women's shoes under his bed. I'm on my way over to the campgrounds to see if Mrs. Harrison can identify them as Bonnie's."

She pulled into the assigned space at the Harrington's trailer next to a dark blue BMW X5. She hesitated before getting out of the car. She looked at the picture on her iPhone. This identification would not only solidify her case, it could very likely upset Mrs. Harrison to see something Bonnie actually wore. There was no easy way to handle this process. She walked up to the door and knocked.

"Mrs. Harrison, I'm Investigator Pickens," she said handing her a business card. "I'm very sorry for your loss. I was wondering if you could identify the shoes in this picture. We think they might belong to Bonnie?"

Before she looked at the picture, Mrs. Harrison invited her into the trailer. The furnishings were like something out of a brochure for an affluent camping magazine. Lots of leather with comfy throws on the furniture and black marble counters and tables as well as accents of gold. Beulah Jean had never seen a trailer look quite so extravagant. There was a man in his seventies sitting on a recliner watching a large screen television in what appeared to be the living area. Mrs. Harrison invited Beulah Jean to sit at the round table with leather seats near the entrance to the trailer.

"We haven't been able to accept Bonnie's death. The last time we saw her she was sitting in the seat you're in just talking up a storm about finishing some necklace she was working on. We only spent three days with her before we got the call that our daughter had gone into early labor. We told her to stay as long as she wanted. She was trying to decide whether she should give Scout another chance and was having difficulty coming to a conclusion. That girl loved the beach and was spending some time each day staring at the ocean. I had hoped she was close to a decision. I can't believe she was killed. There's no evidence here that anything happened to her. Do you know how she died? The detective who told us they found her body didn't say. And now we're told Scout is dead as well. Do you think it was a murder suicide?"

"We're trying to find out how it happened. We don't have enough information yet to answer your question. Everyone is working around the clock to get some answers. I hope we can close the case soon. In the meantime, do you think these belonged to Bonnie?" she asked showing her the picture on the phone.

Mrs. Harrison began sobbing. Her husband came over and held her close. When she lowered her face into his chest, he looked at Beulah Jean and nodded in the affirmative.

"You know, both Bonnie and Scout spent most of their time walking around barefoot," said Mrs. Harrison Either on the beach, around their pottery shop or even once they entered their home. I guess I wasn't surprised when Detective Collins told me they were both found barefoot. I find it interesting Bonnie even had these fancy shoes here in Myrtle Beach. I guess she felt she would be going out more."

"I'm so sorry about this, but we needed a confirmation," said Beulah Jean. "This has been really helpful in solving Bonnie's murder. I'll leave you alone. Please accept my condolences."

Mr. Harrison followed Beulah Jean to her car.

"She has spent the afternoon trying to decide if we should include Scouts body in the memorial service we are planning for Bonnie," he said referring to his wife. "I think it's all been too much for her."

"It's hard for anyone to accept one death, never mind two," said Beulah Jean. "Please let me know if there's anything I can do with the process of getting things arranged with SLED."

"Thank you. That would be helpful. She's been on the phone with them and seems overwhelmed."

"Let me see what I can do to speed the process along, she said getting into her car. She called Detective Collins as she was leaving the campground.

"Can you intervene with SLED for these people," she said as soon as he answered the call. "They just identified the shoes as Bonnie's and the sight of them has shaken Mrs. Harrison to the core."

"I knew she was on the edge when I spoke with her about Mr. Kramer. There's only so much a person can handle. This case asks for above and beyond responses. I'm not sure if it isn't too much for a couple of their age. Are there any other relatives they can rely on?"

"They do have a daughter who delivered a baby recently. Not sure how much help she can give them."

"I'll handle the SLED transfer. Do you know where they want the body to go?"

"They're still trying to decide if they should include Scout in the service. Maybe you should wait until tomorrow to contact them. They need a little time."

"Will do. I spoke with Stone a few minutes ago. He's over at the Hilton Garden Inn waiting to speak with the night clerk."

"I'm on my way to join him. I think we're close to identifying Scout's killer."

"Wait. You mean Bonnie's. Don't You?"

"Maybe. But it definitely wasn't her husband," said Beulah Jean. "Scout was not even in the area when her body was found. She was seeing Max by then. Bonnie's shoes were found under Max's bed. So, my money's on him. But I think there's a good chance we can also finger the man who got to Scout. Hang tight. We should have some answers soon."

"Sounds like you're working the board game and winning. I can't wait for the next report. Stone should fill me in after your meeting."

"Yes. Wish us luck."

Chapter Eighteen

Beulah Jean saw Stone talking to the clerk as soon as she entered the lobby of the Hilton Garden Inn. They saw her approaching and stopped talking.

"Sorry I'm late," she said. "It was difficult leaving my meeting with Mrs. Harrison." She knew Stone would understand what she meant.

"Lefty here was telling me that friend of Max's did stay here for a week," said Stone. "Not surprising, he registered as John Smith and paid cash. He didn't have a rental car. He was picked up by a man the clerk recognized as Max."

"Did he tell you where he was from?" asked Beulah Jean.

"He never said," claimed Lefty. "But when he filled out the registration form, necessary when a person doesn't give us a credit card for incidentals, the address he wrote on the card was in Arizona."

"This is the date he checked out," said Stone showing

Beulah Jean the invoice.

"The same day Scout was found in the mall," she said. "He could probably have walked the block between here and there."

"The daytime clerk told me there was some kind of altercation or fight the night before he checked out," said Beulah Jean. "What can you tell me about it?"

"There were three of them drinking pretty heavy in our bar. As it got closer to midnight, they got louder. A couple of pokes were exchanged. They were pretty intoxicated. Two of them dragged the other one out into the parking lot."

"Did you have any dealings with them after that?"

"No. I never heard any fighting in the parking lot."

"And you never saw them after that?" asked Beulah Jean.

"No. I looked for the discharge invoice when I came in the next day to see if any damage was done. We usually charge the occupant for things like that."

"Was there any damage in the report?" asked Wexler.

"I was surprised. Only one broken glass in the room registered to John Smith, and there was a note about two bloody towels left on the sink in the bathroom," said Lefty.

"We require information like that be recorded by our maids in the case of foul play."

"Do you still have the towels?" asked Beulah Jean.

No. We keep them in a bag on a shelf with the room number attached for forty-eight hours in case there's an inquiry, but I'm afraid they've been thrown away."

Beulah Jean handed Lefty her card. "If you think of anything else, please call my office," she said before asking Detective Stone to meet her in the parking lot when he was finished getting the information he needed for his department.

When he got to her car, she was sitting staring across the grass, looking into the mall parking lot. "Could they have dragged Scout over there and placed him in the rest room hallway?"

"Nah. My guess is they put him in Max's car and drove him over there and waited until the mall was unlocked at six," said Stone.

His phone rang and when he answered he let her know it was Detective Collins. "The lab confirmed Bonnie Kramer's identity," he told Beulah Jean.

"I guess Mrs. Harrison will go forward with the plans

for a memorial service for Bonnie," said Beulah Jean. "When I left there, she was waiting for SLED to release her remains. Her husband said she hadn't decided whether to include Scout in the service. I don't think she blames him for Bonnie's death, but she heard mention of a murder/suicide theory. After what they found under Max's bed, there's no doubt in my mind. I'll call her tonight in case she's still on the fence."

"I'm not sure Collins shares your view," said Stone. "He won't sign off on that until we have Max and his friend – a.k.a. John Smith – or whoever he really is - in custody."

"I got a text from Collins letting me know the owner of the Olive Shop is no longer a person of interest," said Beulah Jean. "But the owners of Seaside Treasures and Kitchen Cutlery remain on the list. What's your reasoning?"

"We still have a sea glass question," said Wexler. We can't be sure where the glass in Scout's hand came from. Maybe after we get these two guys, it will become clear there is no connection. As far as the Kitchen Cutlery, that's a real mess. Wexler's trying to stay on top of all the moving parts."

"I'm going over to give Ellen O'Connell the good news,

said Beulah Jean. "She'll be happy to finally be able to run her shop without being watched like a criminal."

She drove over and parked in the lot near the Olive Shop. The mall was crowded with shoppers. Children's excited voices were heard over the sound of bouncy music at the toddler amusement area. She thought it strange to be among such happy faces while watching for any signs that would lead to solving a murder. Maybe even two.

When she turned the corner leading to the Kitchen Cutlery she nearly bumped into Margie Kane. "I was just going back to my office to call you," she said to Beulah Jean.

"I hope it's good news. I could use a little this morning," said Beulah Jean.

"You'll be happy to know that Dan Logan is back behind the counter at Kitchen Cutlery," said Margie.

"You're kidding. I thought he was having treatment in Houston."

"Dan told me he had three chemo treatments and needs to wait a month before they test him to see if he needs more. He looks a little gray if you ask me but says he's feeling fine. I'm not sure how long he'll keep his shop open.

He wasn't talking much about his future."

"Well, I need to talk with him," said Beulah Jean. "I have several questions that he needs to answer. Maybe he'll be forthcoming when he hears the police still have him on their person of interest list."

"I thought so," said Margie as her eyes grew larger.

Beulah Jean realized she had given away privileged information. There were still a few areas that Margie and her rumor chain didn't know.

"That's why he was one of the merchants who hired me. I assumed they told you."

"I guess I have a reputation for knowing just about everything that goes on at this mall," said Margie. "I'm sure they figured I already knew."

"Thanks for telling me about Dan," said Beulah Jean. "I wouldn't have known about his return. He hasn't kept me abreast of his activities. I'm headed there now." Beulah Jean needed to make sure Dan didn't leave town again before she could question him.

He was sitting in a chair at the back of the store reading some correspondence when she entered his shop. When he saw her coming, he folded his papers and placed them under his right leg.

"Investigator Pickens, I was going to call you later," said Dan.

She didn't believe him but wasn't sure why.

"I was surprised to hear about your medical condition," said Beulah Jean. "Why didn't you let me know you were leaving town?"

"I didn't think I would be gone for more than a couple of days. When I found out I needed to stay longer, I thought the guy taking over for me would fill you in on my condition."

"There's was no one here when I came by. Only a sign saying the shop was closed. What happened?"

"There was a guy who had been trying to convince me to retire for several months," said Dan. "I had bought some products from him. He was anxious to run his own shop and felt this place would work. I had mentioned a couple of times that I wanted to retire. He had all but moved in when I left for my check-up. When I found out I would need to stay in Texas, I called him and asked if he wanted to run the place and eventually transition into taking over."

Beulah Jean pulled the picture of Howard Maxwell out

of her bag. "Is this the man you're referring to?" She showed him the picture of Max and his friend by the pool at the apartment complex.

She could see his reaction was one of surprise.

"Yes. How did you get his picture?"

"That's not important right now," she said locating another picture from her iPhone. "Are these his products?"

"Yes," said Dan. "He's a whittler. I met him at a craft show years ago. He had a booth next to mine. We got talking and he said he hoped to open his own shop someday. Out of the blue, a few months ago, he came into the shop. Said he was moving to the area and wondered if I would put a few of his angels in my shop on consignment."

"Your sister said one of your suppliers was taking over your shop. Is this the man?"

"Well. That was the arrangement. However," he said pulling the papers out from under his leg, "it looks like that won't be happening. He has moved out of town and won't be honoring his agreement."

Dan handed Beulah Jean the papers. She read the short disclaimer from Howard Maxwell. There was no official agreement while Dan was in the hospital, so the letter would be enough to back out of the deal.

"Did you notice the address this was mailed from?" she asked Dan.

He pointed to the waste basket under the counter. "I think I threw it away when I opened the letter."

Beulah Jean went over and found the envelope on top of the trash. She opened the crumpled paper. The postage stamp said, *Santa Monica, CA.*

"Do you have a contact number for Mr. Maxwell?

"I tried calling him just before you arrived," said Dan. "The message says the number is no longer in service."

"What do you make of his sudden change of mind about having his own shop?"

"I'm shocked. He came in almost every day for three weeks when he first moved here. Tried to convince me to retire. Said he would pay me top dollar for my merchandise. Had all these plans to expand by offering more whittled crafts. Could he have been part of the crimes? I'm sick over everything. I don't know what would have made him change his mind."

Beulah Jean was sure she knew. Now to find him.

Chapter Nineteen

Beulah Jean left Dan's shop after making sure he would call her if he heard anything from Howard Maxwell. However, she was convinced that would never happen. Not many people return to the scene of the crime willingly. She was sure he would eventually inform the management at Sovana that he would no longer be renting his apartment. If he even notified them at all. There was no way for them to serve him with a court document suing him for breach of contract. If things were running true to form, his Venice Beach address would probably be vacated. She had covered these cases before. The trail was long, and the chase was difficult. Her priority was to clear her clients' names. One down, two to go. She walked over to the Olive Shop.

"Good news, Ellen," said Beulah Jean. "You're no longer on the person of interest list. No more looking over your shoulder. I'm sorry it took this long, but things became complicated."

"Oh, happy day. I can breathe again. Have you told Brandy and Dan the good news?" asked Ellen. "I saw Dan this morning. He's looking a little green. Could use some cheering up."

"Actually, their news isn't as good. I'm still working on clearing their names."

"I knew that sea glass would be a problem for Brandy," said Ellen. "But what's holding Dan's release?"

"It's complicated," said Beulah Jean. "That man who was going to take over his shop when he was in the hospital has become a person of interest. His relationship to Dan is still unclear. Until we can sort things out, Dan remains on the top of the list."

There was nothing else she could say without compromising the investigation. "My next invoice will only go to Brandy and Dan. I'm happy I was able to take your name off my client list."

Beulah Jean walked to the back wall of the shop and returned with three bottles. "I did want to buy more of my favorite olive oil. I'm looking forward to a long weekend down on the Isle of Palms and wanted to bring some along."

"How did your friend like that last bottle?"

"He loved it. That's why I'm sure he'll be delighted with my choice. What do I owe you?"

"These are on the house," she said as she wrapped the bottles and placed them in a bag. "Just having my name off the watch list is worth more than the cost of this olive oil. Thanks, Beulah Jean. I hope you're able to do the same for Brandy and Dan soon."

"That's the plan," said Beulah Jean as she took the bag of oil from Ellen and walked out of the store.

Ten minutes later she was entering the KOA Campgrounds. The BMW was still parked in the same spot near the Harrisons' trailer. Beulah Jean pulled up next to their car and parked. Mr. Harrison opened the trailer door when he saw her get out of her car.

"How is she doing?" asked Beulah Jean.

"She's had a tough day," he said. "I think she's doing better since she made the decision to include Scout in the memorial service. Come in. She's talking with our daughter about the arrangements."

They both walked into the trailer as Mrs. Harrison was saying goodbye to her daughter.

"Hello, Ms. Pickens. Would you like a cup of coffee?" said Mrs. Harrison.

"I'd love one. How are you doing?"

"I still can't believe our Bonnie is gone," she said pouring coffee for the three of them. "And Scout. I knew they were having problems, but I never imagined they would both be dead. Detective Collins said they were no longer thinking he was responsible for Bonnie's death. Do they have someone in custody? Is it the same person who killed Scout?"

Beulah Jean wasn't sure how much information she could share. Things were so unsettled. "They don't have anyone in custody at this time, but there is a warrant out for the arrest of Bonnie's suspected killer. I'm so sorry for your loss. The identity of Scout's killer is still unclear. But things are moving in the right direction. I hope the case will be solved very soon."

Mrs. Harrison went into her bedroom and returned with an 8X10 photo from Bonnie and Scout's wedding. "I pulled this out of my box of family photos this afternoon. The man at the funeral home asked if I had a picture for the service."

Who have you decided to use for the service?" asked Beulah Jean.

"McMillan-Small Funeral Home & Crematory over on 67th Avenue," said Mrs. Harrison. "Detective Collins said he would arrange for both bodies to be sent there so we can hold the service next Monday. I know they don't have a burial plot, so I'm having them cremated. I'm looking into a columbarium close by."

"Will your daughter be coming for the service?"

"Yes. She will probably be the only one. Her husband was given a leave from duty in the army for the recent birth of their daughter, so he won't be able to join her."

"I was wondering if you want me to call Seth, their best man at their wedding," asked Beulah Jean. "He's been very helpful to our investigation. And I know he's pretty devastated by their deaths. He was quite close to them up in Seagrove."

"Of course," said Mrs. Harrison. "I'd forgotten all about Seth. He was a good friend. Bonnie's maid of honor was my daughter. There were no other attendants in their wedding. I think they have some friends in North Carolina."

"I'd be happy to call Seth and give him the details," said Beulah Jean.

"Thank you so much. The service is scheduled for 1:00 p.m. on Monday. Are you sure it's no trouble?"

"No trouble at all," said Beulah Jean. "I'll be on my way. You have a lot of loose ends to tie up. I'll see you on Monday."

Beulah Jean hugged Mrs. Harrison before she left. She had forgotten what it felt like to hold an older body close. Her grandmother died five years go. She could feel the bones in Mrs. Harrison's back and a tremble that seemed to run throughout her body. It was hard to imagine what it felt like to be told out of the blue that a loved one, rather two loved ones, had died. She put her empty coffee cup in the sink and walked out of the trailer.

Miss Shelby was so happy to see Beulah Jean that she bumped into the office desk in her attempt to greet her master. "Hey there girl," said Beulah Jean. "Are you ready for our trip down to the Isle of Palms?" Her golden retriever was the best passenger on those long trips. Leaning her head out of the passenger window was her favorite way to travel.

Beulah Jean picked up the suitcase she had packed the night before and loaded the cooler with her special pineapple and lemon cake she promised Jack she'd bring.

After making sure Miss Shelby took care of her needs, she put her in the car along with her bags and they were on their way.

As soon as she passed Pawleys Island on Route 17 south, she called Seth from her cell phone.

"It's Beulah Jean Pickens," she said when he answered the phone. "I thought you'd want to know they're having a memorial service for Bonnie and Scout on Monday afternoon at 1:00. Thought maybe you'd want to attend."

"Damn right, I do," said Seth. "I need to see the body to prove my best friend is actually dead."

"Well. I'm not sure that will work. Bonnie's aunt is having both he and Bonnie cremated."

"Of course, I wasn't thinking. They never talked about buying a burial plot. At our age, that conversation is not on the top of our list. Where is the service?"

"The funeral home is on Route 17 Bypass and 67th

Avenue in Myrtle Beach," said Beulah Jean. "Called McMillan-Small. Is there anyone else you can think of to notify? I'm sure you know most of their friends."

"Yes. I'll take care of all that. I'll see you on Monday. Have a good weekend."

"Thanks, Seth. See you Monday."

Before she knew it, she was pulling into Jack's circular driveway. The Spanish Moss hanging from the tree in his front yard as the sun was beginning to set was a warm and welcoming sight. Miss Shelby put her paws on the edge of the door with her head hanging out the window. This was becoming one of her favorite spots. Seeing Jack walk out of his house caused her to wag her tail back and forth brushing Beulah Jean's arm. When he opened the door, she ran through his legs and circled twice, then went off toward the Intracoastal Waterway in his backyard.

"Hey, Babe," said Jack walking around to Beulah Jean's side of the car. "Am I glad to see you." She nearly jumped into his arms. Something she'd been looking forward to for the entire ride south.

"Can we just stay like this in suspended animation for

the entire weekend?" she asked.

He swayed their two bodies back and forth like they were in the middle of a ballroom dance before he stopped dead and whispered, "Hold that thought until I get you inside. I have a surprise."

He brought her bags into his bedroom and went to the kitchen to pour them glasses of wine. Then they walked out the back door to the boathouse down by his dock and sat watching the boats moving south as the sun continued to set.

"Now, about that surprise," said Jack. He pulled an envelope from his pocket and handed it to Beulah Jean.

She took out two plane tickets to Hyannis, a reservation confirmation for two tickets on the Hy-Line high-speed ferry from Hyannis to Nantucket, and the confirmation for four nights at the White Elephant Resort on Nantucket Island. She took a deep breath. Just what the doctor ordered.

"This is a wonderful surprise," she said. "I wasn't sure it would all come together. Just the thought of Thanksgiving on Nantucket calms my entire body."

She kissed him and then rested her head on his shoulder. She brought him up to date on the Kramer's cases and they sipped their wine and enjoyed the scenery until darkness fell and forced them into his cottage.

"I forgot to tell you," he said, placing the seafood platter on the dining room table along with another bottle of wine. "The rest of the surprise. To make sure nothing gets in the way of our trip, I'm taking the next two weeks off to help you tie up all the loose ends necessary to clear your clients' names from these murders. Of course, I'll need to stay in Market Common at your place until things resolve."

"You never cease to amaze me," she said. "How can I ever thank you?"

"Finish dinner and I'll think of a way," he said with a smile from ear to ear.

Chapter Twenty

Beulah Jean couldn't believe the number of cars parked in the lot outside of the funeral home. She and Jack signed the visitor's register and walked up to the front of the chapel where the ashes of Bonnie and Scout Kramer were held in matching urns, with a lovely spray of fall flowers between them. In front of the flowers was the wedding picture which had been placed in a bronze frame.

The Harrisons were sitting in the front row of the chapel. Beulah Jean introduced Jack and met Hanna, their daughter, who was holding a sleeping baby. She could see the resemblance between Hanna and her father.

"I can't believe how many people have driven here for the service," said Mrs. Harrison. "I guess they did have some good times in their marriage."

"From the looks of this crowd," said Beulah Jean, "they shared many good years throughout their North Carolina life." She could see Seth sitting a few rows back.

She was surprised to see Brandy Sommers and Ellen O'Connell sitting across the aisle. Sitting next to Ellen was Margie Kane. Beulah Jean assumed she was there to make sure she had complete confirmation of the final resting place for the two bodies formerly resting at her place of employment. After all, she would be taking all the details to her gossip committee back at the mall.

The music ended and Beulah Jean and Jack found a seat. Detectives Stone and Wexler came out from a door up near the front of the chapel and walked to the back of the room. They made sure to take in the faces in the crowd as they passed.

She knew they were hoping to find answers still outstanding in the two cases of murder.

The minister came out of the same front door and walked up to the Harrisons. He offered his condolences and then went to the podium in the front of the chapel. His prayers and message were delivered as if he knew the Kramer's their entire lives. Beulah Jean knew he had met with the Harrisons over the weekend and was sure Mrs. Harrison had regaled him with stories of her niece.

The minister asked if anyone wished to offer any memories of the deceased. Beulah Jean watched as Seth moved up to the podium along with two other friends.

"He was one of my best buddies," said Seth. "I was his best man. We spent time together in the service and when we got back home, hardly a day would go by without a visit from Scout. I know he had some tough times and there was a period when I didn't think he and Bonnie would survive his PTSD episodes. Then, when he came back from rehab this last time, he was like the old Scout. I was sure they could work things out. They just needed more time." His voice cracked. "Just a little more time." He wasn't able to speak anymore.

The older man standing on Seth's right put his arm around Seth and the man on his left went to the podium.

"Scout was in my whittling group. We all needed something when we got back from Afghanistan. Scout got us interested in whittling. We would meet once a week and solve the problems of the world as we scraped the wood and molded it into something that would make us proud. When he made his first angel, he said he found his way out of darkness. He must have made four or five each day for a month. His angels sold the most from our table at the craft show. I can't believe he's gone. I hope he's up there with the real angels."

A woman walked up from the back of the chapel. When she turned around, Beulah Jean recognized her from the pottery museum in Seagrove, North Carolina.

"Bonnie was the nicest potter in our group. She was always there when anyone needed anything. She had recently developed an interest in sea glass. Wanted to put in on every piece in her shop. Finally settled for using the glass in most of her jewelry, cutting and polishing the pieces to fit her designs. She will be missed in Seagrove. May she rest in peace." She walked over to offer her condolences to the Harrisons before returning to her seat.

The older man who had put his arm around Seth came forward. "The Kramer's were my next-door neighbors. If you call five acres next door. I could always count on them for anything I needed. When I broke my arm a few years ago, Scout mowed my five acres for three months without taking a dime for his efforts. And Bonnie, she sent over meals every week until my cast came off. She had been friends with my wife before she passed."

The three men walked back to their seats as the minister

went back to the podium.

"There seems to be a lot of love in this room for those two," he said pointing toward the urns. "Let us bow our heads and pray."

The service ended and people began walking out to their cars. Seth asked Beulah Jean if he could talk with her outside. She went up to the Harrisons and told them she would keep them informed of the case as things became known. Stone and Wexler stopped her on her way out and said they had new information. She and Jack followed them into one of the smaller rooms further down the lobby. She introduced Jack and they sat in the corner of the room.

"You were right about your theory that Howard Maxwell would leave Venice Beach," said Stone. "We heard from the Santa Monica Police that the place looks empty. No forwarding address. No neighbors saw him in the last two months."

"No," said Beulah Jean, "because he was here in Myrtle Beach, living at Sovana. What about his friend, the famous 'John Smith?'"

"They're checking him out now. One of the members of the crime scene unit thinks he looks like someone who spent time for assault. We're waiting for a confirmation."

"That sounds promising," said Jack. "If they can identify him, he could turn them on to Maxwell's whereabouts."

"Nothing ever seems to be that easy," said Wexler. "We'll keep you posted. We released Kramer's car to his friend who spoke earlier. He's taking it back to North Carolina."

"Thanks," said Beulah Jean. "I'm going to speak with Seth now."

All four walked outside together. Beulah Jean and Jack walked over to where Seth was standing talking to several friends.

"I hear you're taking Scout's car back," said Beulah Jean.

"Yeah. My friend, Mike is driving my car. I have to go to the impound lot to get Scouts. But I was hoping we could talk. I need to know where you're at in finding his killer."

Beulah Jean felt sorry for Seth. He actually looked like he just lost his best friend.

"Why don't you come with us over to my office in Market Common," she said. "We can take you over to the impound lot after dinner."

"Thanks. That would be great. I'm climbing the walls over this killing. Can't get any sleep. Maybe there's something I can do to help."

Beulah Jean didn't think there was anything he could do, but she wanted to help him through this period of depression. He got into Jack's back seat, and they drove to her office.

Miss Shelby greeted them with her usual enthusiasm, and they let her out to take care of her needs. In record time, she was back at the door. Her treat, as usual, was the only thing on her mind. That golden retriever had her priorities.

They sat around Beulah Jean's desk as she pulled out her file on each of the Kramer's cases. She placed some of the notes on her desk and started to fill Seth in about the arrest of Howard Maxwell.

"Wait," said Seth. "I know him."

"You know *this* Howard Maxwell?" she asked showing Seth the picture taken poolside at Sovana.

"Yes. And I know the man standing next to him."

"Wait. What is that man's name?"

"Max called him Fitz. I think his name was Fitzgerald. He's from Venice Beach in California."

Beulah Jean could hardly get the words out.

"How do you know these guys?"

"Max met Scout at a craft show a couple years ago. He came to Seagrove to visit him and Bonnie. One time he brought Fitz with him. They all came to the brewery one night. Max had a real crush on Bonnie. We all saw how he couldn't take his eyes off her. Scout didn't seem to notice."

"I'm trying to digest the fact that Max knew Bonnie before their meeting in Myrtle Beach," said Beulah Jean. "So, he didn't just meet her and fall all over her immediately. He had a thing for her. How did he know where to find her?"

"I'm not sure," said Seth. "But he did come to the brewery with Scout one night after Bonnie left him. I'm sure Scout told him he thought she went to Myrtle Beach. He didn't know where in Myrtle, but he was sure she was somewhere down here."

Beulah Jean looked at Jack. "Are you thinking what I'm thinking."

He smiled. "How would you like to take a trip with us

to the west coast?" he asked Seth.

"I would be all over that. If he's responsible for Bonnie's death, I'd like the first crack at him."

"We couldn't allow that," said Beulah Jean. "But you would be able to flaunt the fact that you uncovered this mystery and found Bonnie's killer."

She wasn't sure he would settle for anything less than attacking Maxwell, but it was a chance she was willing to take. Especially since Jack would be there to help restrain Seth.

"I'm going to call Detective Collins and let him know our plans. I'll tell him you'll pick up Scouts car when we return from California."

"I'll make the plane reservations and get us rooms in Santa Monica," said Jack.

"Is there a T.J. Maxx in the area?" asked Seth. "I'm gonna need a change of clothes or two for this trip."

"Not a problem," said Beulah Jean. "I'll take you there and when we get back let's grab a bite to eat." She looked over at Jack who was on the phone. "When you finish with the reservations, take Miss Shelby and walk down to the outdoor patio at Toffinos. We'll meet you there."

Chapter Twenty-One

The plane bounced twice before finally landing at LAX. The Santa Ana winds troubled the pilots. They had been known to create intense turbulence and wind shear. There are records of the winds flipping small planes. Even one of the 747's like the one they were in had dropped a thousand feet by the force. Beulah Jean was happy when they finally taxied on the runway.

They claimed their bags and picked up their rental car before driving less than ten miles north to the Hotel Shangri-La on Ocean Avenue in Santa Monica. Their rooms had spectacular views of the Santa Monica Pier with its famous Ferris Wheel and magnificent sunsets. They decided to walk across to the street and grab a bite to eat at Maria Sol, the Mexican Restaurant at the end of the Pier. It was time to decide on a plan to find Howard Maxwell.

They ordered Cadillac Margaritas and shared a Puerto Neuvo Lobster Plate. It was hard to keep their minds on the task at hand. The strong winds kept them inside, watching the white caps through the curved glass window. No one was brave enough to sit on the outside patio that close to the water during the wrath of a Santa Ana.

"I think when we finish here, we should get our car and drive down Ocean Avenue toward Marina del Rey," said Jack. "The fifteen-minute ride will take us along southern Santa Monica and into Venice Beach."

"We can check out the address Detective Collins gave me for Howard Maxwell," said Beulah Jean. "He's arranged for the local police to let us into his condo tomorrow afternoon, but it wouldn't hurt to see if there are any lights on at night. Maybe someone is using the place while he's gone."

"In the morning, we can walk Venice Beach and talk to some of the locals," said Jack. "They might have some information leading to Maxwell's arrest.

"I'd like to walk alone," said Seth. "I think if we separate, we might not be as overwhelming to these residents. I've been here before and there are quite a few characters lining the walkway along the beach. They're a different breed of artists. From women who create scenery on canvas with seashells, to fortune tellers, street vendors and performers on wheels. Each week new people who call themselves artists line up along side famous artists for the tourists to purchase one-of-a-kind pieces to bring home."

Walking back along the Santa Monica pier, they passed a crowd of college students taking advantage of the amusements after a day of classes. The lines stretched back to the street with people waiting for every ride except the Ferris wheel. No one was tempting fate

They got their car out of the hotel garage and drove along Ocean Avenue. They could tell as soon as they crossed into Venice Beach. The dwellings were more like beach cottages and much closer together. They took a right at the light in the center of town and found themselves looking at a deserted Muscle Beach. Famous for years for the stunt men and acrobats performing in the thirties and forties, now this section of beach was the go-to place for gymnasts, weightlifters, and bodybuilders. There were also those who just wanted to show off their physique. The locals counted Max and his friend Fitz among the latter.

The morning crowds had left the sand in need of raking.

Two young Mexican men worked the roped off section in an attempt to prepare the area with all the exercise equipment for the next day.

After watching the men ready the space, they rode south into Marina del Rey. The upscale neighborhood lined the canal with homes fit for millionaires. The change in housing made them wonder how the Venice Beach residents were able to purchase their properties for such bargains.

They came back to their hotel after driving along the Third Street Promenade, the noted shopping area lined with boutiques and restaurants serving visitors and locals alike. The change in time zone forced them to head back to the Shangri-La for much needed sleep. The day ahead was full of hope and promise.

Breakfast was served on the veranda warmed by the morning sunlight. Finally, the winds had changed direction. After her second cup of coffee, Beulah Jean went over the agenda they agreed to for the day. Seth left first after agreeing to meet them at the restaurant across from the Muscle Beach area for lunch. He was certain someone would know how to find Max and Fitz. And he was on a mission to be the one to find them.

Jack and Beulah Jean parked their car along a side street on the Santa Monica line. The beach was already crowded with tourists and the local regulars. Skaters and boarders weaved among the walkers. Crafters had their wares set on blankets along the cement walkway on the edge of the beach. Fortune tellers, glassblowers and seashell artists all fought for the attention of the passersby. When the cartoon artist asked if they wanted a picture for a souvenir, Beulah Jean turned the request into an investigation.

"Have you ever drawn pictures of either of these men?" she asked showing him the picture of Max and Fitz.

He jolted back when he saw the picture. "I'd never get any money out of either of them," said the artist continuing to set up his easel.

"What makes you think that? Do you know these men?"

"Most people around here know them. They have a reputation. We leave them alone. We don't bother them, and they don't bother us."

"What kind of reputation?" asked Beulah Jean.

"They've both done time. They boast about it down on Muscle Beach. They're hustlers. Anywhere they can get a dime. Most of the women are warned not to play their games."

Beulah Jean wished Bonnie had been warned. Maybe she'd be alive today.

"This guy," said Jack pointing to Max's friend. "What can you tell me about him?"

"Not a nice guy," said the artist. "Likes the women. Got in trouble for using them. Assault, they called it. I'd call it rape and drape. He likes his body and wants to show them how he uses every muscle."

"Does he have a name?" asked Beulah Jean.

"He's been called a lot of things. Not sure what his official name is on paper. Heard him called Fitz. Others call him Crazy Ike. Some have heard him referred to as Mr. Helium. I think it has something to do with the Muscle Beach reputation."

"Any idea where he lives?" asked Jack.

"He was rooming with the guy in that picture for a few months after he got out of jail. There's a girl on the top floor of that aqua and pink townhouse on the edge of town. She gives him meals on occasion. I think he sleeps there at times. Don't think he has a permanent residence. Not in this area, at least. He disappears often. Maybe he has a real address in another state. Got me."

"Thanks for your help," said Beulah Jean. They needed to continue down the beach asking more of the local craft's people for information. By the time they reached the Muscle Beach area they were late for their lunch meeting with Seth.

He was seated at an outside table at Figtree's Café watching the activity along the beach. They joined him and ordered lunch before Seth brought them up to date with his morning discovery.

"I wasted no time getting the information we need," said Seth. "I cornered a guy on Muscle Beach. He knew Max and Fitz. The guy's name is Fitzgerald. Maurice Fitzgerald. Popular with the boys who like to make trouble. He's been in jail twice for assault. Somehow, he never learns. But that's not the information I found most interesting."

"What do you mean?" asked Beulah Jean.

"Well. This guy tells me the last time Fitz got out of jail he was boasting about how his cellmate taught him how to get rid of the women without getting caught for the act."

"You mean murder?" asked Jack.

"Exactly. He said Fitz learned if you get the woman

drunk enough and lay her down next to a plastic garbage bag, eventually she rolls over and smothers herself without leaving evidence of a strangulation. And, if she doesn't roll over on her own, you can place the bag on her face for less than a minute with a little pressure. Works every time. His cellmate managed to do away with four women using that process."

"I don't believe it," said Jack. "The coroner would be able to find the evidence during an autopsy?"

"According to Fitz, the only sign would be tiny specks of blood on the lungs. Something the coroner wouldn't normally list as a cause of death."

"Oh my god, Jack," said Beulah Jean. "We found several rolled up garbage bags on Howard Maxwell's closet floor. We nearly threw them out. I think Stone has them in the evidence locker. Maybe he can have the coroner examine them?"

She walked out to the sidewalk and made a call to Detective Collins. When she returned their lunch had arrived.

"He's skeptical, but says he'll call the medical examiner. Any shot in the dark is worth checking at this point. Both deaths are still listed as undetermined."

They finished lunch and left to meet the Santa Monica Police at Howard Maxwell's Venice Beach condo.

The condo parking was in the back alley. They walked around to the front across from the beach. The green palms lined the white wrought iron stairwell to the entrance on the second floor. From the outside, it looked like the place was closed up tight. White heavy sheer pleated curtains covered the windows leaving the room dark inside.

They could tell immediately that the place had recently been occupied. The two bedrooms had towels on the floor and the beds were unmade. There were coffee grounds on the counter near the coffee maker. The filter was still wet. Someone had used the appliance within the last few days. Except for the bedclothes, no personal belongings could be found anywhere in the condo.

"We understand the place is up for sale," said Officer Higgins. He could tell they wondered why all the drawers and closets were empty.

"Do you know if a local realtor has the listing?" asked Beulah Jean. "Maybe they'll have a phone number or address where Max is staying."

"We only know it's for sale because the neighbors two doors down told us," said Higgins. "They didn't know who had the listing. They think Max had a buyer and didn't need to list the property."

"Did they mention this guy Fitz being here with Max?" asked Beulah Jean showing the officer the picture.

"You talking about Maurice?" asked the officer.

"This guy has more names than the McDonald's menu," said Beulah Jean.

She pointed to Fitz. "This is the man I'm asking about. He's a person of interest in one of the murders in Myrtle Beach."

"Yeah. That's Maurice Fitzgerald. Middle name Trouble as far as we're concerned. He's been around this area for years. In and out of prison. Most of the locals have experienced his crazy antics. We've been looking for him since Detective Collins put out the warrant. Our feelers are out. I'm sure he'll turn up sooner or later. He always does."

Seth walked outside and headed for Muscle Beach. He wasn't satisfied with the answer from Officer Higgins. He knew someone would have the information he needed.

There were five guys working out on the equipment on

Muscle Beach. Seth took off his t-shirt and moved closer to the guy lifting weights. "You look like you've been lifting those for some time," said Seth. "Like you could handle that weight with only one arm. Do you come here daily?"

"Without fail," said the weightlifter. "I train for my weekend matches."

"Where are they held?" he asked.

"Mostly in Chula Vista, in the San Diego area."

"Do you know if this guy competes in those matches?" asked Seth, showing him a picture of Fitz.

"Fitz competes anywhere he can make a dime," said the weightlifter.

"I tried to find him last night," said Seth. "Do you know if he's out of town?"

The weightlifter got up and changed the weights on the ends of his bar.

"He works the southern circuit, mostly San Diego. I think he has a place on Pacific Beach. The money pays nightly in that area of the state. He also has a place down on the Mexico's Baja peninsula. Rosarito Beach, I think. I haven't seen him in over a week. My guess is he's down there."

"Thanks for the info," said Seth. He couldn't wait to get back to Beulah Jean.

She and Jack were leaving Max's condo. Seth was out of breath when he reached the car in the back alley.

"You look like you had a run in with a seagull and lost," said Jack.

"I think I won," said Seth.

They got in the car and Jack started driving back to Santa Monica. Seth relayed the information he managed to get from the weightlifter.

"This is turning into an international incident," said Beulah Jean. "I'm not sure what authority we'll have if those guys cross the border. We might have hit a dead end."

"I'm not giving up that easy," said Seth. "Scout was my best friend. I'm going to Pacific Beach."

Beulah Jean knew her limitations as a private investigator. She had the authority to search for murderers, but the arrest would have to come from the authorities in charge of the jurisdiction. She needed to talk with Detective Collins.

The call came to their Santa Monica hotel within hours of Beulah Jean's call to Collins. He had made arrangements with the FBI to work with Beulah Jean and Jack in their search and possible capture of the two fugitives at large. They would meet the agents and a couple of U.S. Marshalls tomorrow at 233 West Broadway in San Diego.

Chapter Twenty-Two

After spending a sleepless night, Beulah Jean, Jack, and Seth forfeited breakfast in the hotel. They ordered coffee and bagels to go and checked out early in order to get on the road. Making it to San Diego before the appointed meeting time with the FBI Agents was their goal. Beulah Jean decided to drive. She had the lead foot.

Seth had a few addresses in Pacific Beach where the weightlifter from Muscle Beach had given him, along with an address for three match sites in Chula Vista. But he had an idea the two on the run would not go to either of those locations because there was a powerlifting competition scheduled for tomorrow in Del Mar. The prize money at the fairgrounds was the most given at any recent event.

He knew Fitz was looking for more cash. From what he had detected while gathering information from the Muscle Beach crowd, Fitz used Max's money like it was his own.

There had to be something Fitz held over Max. Maybe they did do time together. Who knew what kind of information men shared in close quarters?

Once they were on Route 5 heading south, their coffee woke up their senses and their conversation picked-up.

"I spent several hours last night online trying to learn as much about these powerlifting competitions as possible," said Seth. "The Del Mar Fairgrounds would be my best bet for finding these guys," as he went on to explain why.

"Collins set up our meeting for noon in San Diego," said Beulah Jean. "He also texted me last night to say Stone and Wexler will be flying in to join us. How far are the fairgrounds from the meeting location?"

"I'm looking at the location on my iPhone right now," said Jack. "Looks like we pass Del Mar about twenty-five minutes before the San Diego International Airport. Maybe we can call the agents and see if the meeting could be changed to the airport, and when Stone and Wexler land, we could fill them all in and make a decision… Del Mar or one of the two San Diego sites."

"My vote is for Del Mar," said Seth.
Beulah Jean heard the determination in his voice and his

need to take out Max for killing his best friend. She felt Seth would try to sneak away from the authorities as soon as he saw an opportunity – something she shared with Jack the night before when neither of them could sleep. She was confident Jack would handle Seth.

"The number Collins gave me for our FBI contacts is in my phone," she said. "Jack, will you call and see if they can meet us at the airport?"

"On it," he replied.

The nearly two-hour drive south took them by Laguna Beach, San Juan Capistrano where each year the swallows returned and of course, LaJolla, the scene of the annual Torrey Pines PGA Golf Tournament. The scenery was beautiful and on any other occasion Beulah Jean would have stopped several times to enjoy the spectacular sites. But time was not on their side.

They arrived at Terminal B in time to greet Stone and Wexler when they deplaned. Two of the four agents who had been assigned to assist in this capture were already at the baggage claim and introduced themselves as the party gathered. Introductions were made all around and a meeting location already arranged by the agents, was ready for them next to the Southwest Airlines Lounge.

It took less than a half hour to brief the FBI agents and share the information Seth had managed to pull together overnight with Stone and Wexler. Everyone agreed the Del Mar site would be the most likely attraction to Fitz. They learned that two other agents were stationed near the border into Tijuana – a very busy border crossing used often by Fitz and Max on their way to another of Max's properties in Rosarita Beach. Stone had done a pretty good background check on Max and all his aliases. Seemed as though he had family money and was enjoying depleting as much of it as possible.

They drove the twenty-five minutes north to Del Mar and checked into the Winners Circle Resort. After dropping off their bags in their rooms, they met up at the Seabiscuit Skybox for a late lunch and decision making.

They studied a map of the area and the agents pointed out the exits and camera locations from their vantage point on the top floor.

The competition would be taking place in O'Brien Hall. The problem was the place held over 6,000 spectators. Most of the activity would be completed in the middle of the hall. Stations of equipment are spread out like any Olympic event and lifters would be competing at the same time – drawing the attention of the spectators back and forth.

After hearing about Seth's conversation with the guys from Venice Beach, Beulah Jean agreed that Fitz would want to compete in the powerlifting competition because it brought in a larger payoff.

"What's the difference, Seth?" asked Stone.

"From what I read, weightlifters perform two lifts – the snatch, and the clean & jerk. Powerlifters perform three lifts – the back squat, the bench press and the deadlift."

"I imagine it's the money that leads one to the powerlifting competition," said Stone. "What kind of cash are we talking?"

"First place in the 50+ category takes $40,000," said Seth.

"Fitz will need more than one win to stay afloat hiding away for long," said Wexler.

"Not if he keeps Max close," said Stone. "That guy seems to grow money."

Beulah Jean noticed Jack staring at Seth. "How did you

get so smart about this topic overnight?" Jack asked Seth. "Do you use research in your career? I never asked what you do for a living back in Seagrove."

"I write for the Veteran's Administration. My job in the service was with the Public Affairs Office where I handled a great deal of correspondence. When I got out, they approached me about using my skills to add to their newsletters and pamphlets that get sent to all the vets. It keeps me out of trouble and makes me feel as though I'm still contributing to the cause. I was hoping to be able to write a real novel about our experience in Afghanistan. All I have are boxes of notes. Maybe someday."

Beulah Jean understood now why Seth seemed so driven to help solve this case. It was a lot more than just revenge for his best friend.

"So, let's agree on our locations for the meet tomorrow," said Beulah Jean. "I don't know about you, but I'm exhausted just hearing about the lifting. We probably should all take some time to case the grounds and make sure we know where the contestants will be at all times."

They agreed on the time and meeting place for the next day's competition. Seth left first, nearly tripping over his own feet. Beulah Jean reminded Jack of her concerns. She didn't want to have to regret allowing him this close to her case. Things could get very real, and people could get hurt.

"Babe," said Jack. "He's been looking for a way to accept what happened to his best friends. He's so far into this now, there's no stopping him. Don't worry. I've got it."

O'Brien Hall was packed. The first match went thirty-five minutes. No sign of either Max or Fitz. Everyone had stayed within a few feet of their assigned locations, properly using their communication system in order to hear and speak to one another, except Seth. He walked the perimeter of the bench press area five or six times at Beulah Jean's last count. Jack was not letting him out of his sight. The crowd roared when the first competition ended. Neither Max nor Fitz took part in that meet. Beulah Jean was beginning to wonder if they had put all their eggs in the wrong basket. What if it turned up empty? Maybe they should have looked more carefully at the meets in Chula Vista or Pacific Beach.

"Three o'clock on the south stairs." The voice was Stone's. They all heard him and saw a man looking like Fitz walking down the stairs to the competition floor.

Beulah Jean saw Wexler moving closer to that section of seating. She could also see one of the FBI agents guiding people away from the exterior double doors that would allow access to the outside. He would close that off as an escape route. Her adrenaline moved quicker than she expected as her eyes darted across the hall, looking for any sign of Max. A quick flash of light moved in the corner of her left eye. There he was. Walking under the bleachers. He must have seen Seth. She started to head in his direction - then stopped. Over her right shoulder she saw Fitz looking for Max. His eyes scanned the entire arena. Then he saw him. Max was running. Heading for the door at the opposite end of the hall, farthest from the competition Fitz would be entering. She could tell Fitz had frozen in place. Within seconds Wexler had moved close enough to grab Fitz. The FBI agent came up from behind and cuffed him.

"Nine o'clock," said Jack, as the door opened, and he followed Max outside the hall. "He's heading toward the off-track betting facility."

"Where's Seth, Jack?" asked Beulah Jean.

"Lost him."

For the next ten minutes, there was very little interaction among the agents or anyone else working the takedown. It was hard to keep up. Beulah Jean had moved outside and was aware of the number of police cars filling the parking lot. Guns were drawn and agents were covering all corners of the grounds.

That's when she saw Jack standing to the left of the betting facility, outside the door of the dressing rooms used by the competitors. She knew what was happening. By the time she caught up to him the act had been complete. He opened the door and Seth stumbled out. Face bloodied and shirt ripped. Then Jack went in and pulled Max off the floor, placed his hands behind his back and used his handcuffs to hold him there until the FBI agent arrived.

"Nice work," said the agent as he took Max from Jack. "My partner has taken the other one into custody. Let's give this guy the same fifty-cent ride." He looked at Seth.

"Are you okay, buddy?"

"Never better," said Seth.

Stone and Wexler went with the FBI agents to book Max and Fitz. They would accompany that escort back to South Carolina as soon as their extradition could be arranged.

After Seth cleaned himself up, he joined Beulah Jean and Jack in the lounge back at the Winners Circle Resort.

"Feeling satisfied?" asked Jack.

"Not really, but I took the edge off. I'll never be able to feel like Max has been punished enough to account for the deaths of my best friend and his wife. Not even if he gets the death penalty. But I really appreciate how you let me feel a small part of that punishment."

Beulah Jean ordered drinks and appetizers for the table and left the room to make a call to Detective Collins.

"Congratulations Investigator Pickens," said Collins when he answered the phone. "You've done it again. I hope you know how far your star rises every time you close one of these cases. I'm going to continue to convince you to leave that business of yours in Market Common and come to work for us."

"Your persistence is commendable, detective. But I'm very happy with my life as a private investigator."

"Speaking of private investigators, I gave your name to

one of our residents. She owns the East Shores Campground along the Grand Strand. She called me today for some advice. It appears as though someone is starting fires on the grounds. No one has been hurt, yet. But she's afraid one day her whole place will be on fire."

"Sounds like it could be serious," said Beulah Jean.

"Yeah. That's why I gave her your name. She'll be in touch to see if she can hire you."

"I'll be on Nantucket for the next few days to celebrate the holiday. And who knows, maybe I'll like it enough to stay. Happy Thanksgiving, Detective.

Carole O'Neill

Epilogue

They sat in front of the fireplace, still feeling full from the special 2:00 p.m. Thanksgiving Feast the White Elephant served in the Brandt Point Grill. Their walk along the cobblestoned street downtown allowed time to digest the meal as they admired the window decorations designed for the holidays. Music drew them to the Club Car Bar housed in a train from the original Nantucket Railroad. After sipping on Bailey's Irish Crème, they headed back to their suite with the view of the water. Beulah Jean felt warm all over. The staff sent an elegant tray of strawberries with whipped cream to their room along with the bottle of champagne they were slowly sipping.

"I could get used to this," said Beulah Jean.

"Just say the word and it's yours," said Jack.

"You're not ready to give up your career at this point, are you?" asked Beulah Jean.

"No, but who says we have to continue working in the low country. If this place makes you happy, I would be willing to change the scenery for this. At least for a little while. Why not?"

"I would miss your lovely cottage and surroundings on the Isle of Palms," said Beulah Jean.

"You know I love you and want whatever makes you happy," said Jack. "Any island. Pick an island."

"I'm enjoying the private investigator work. Especially when we can work together. Have you given any thought to leaving the Police Department on the Isle of Palms?"

"I think we could discuss several options, if you're serious," said Jack.

Beulah Jean's phone pinged. There was a message from Detective Collins.

"What do you think he wants on Thanksgiving?"

She read the message and walked over to the window, just staring far out at the incoming ferry. Jack moved to her and put his arms around her.

"What is it, Babe?"

"Let's not ruin this special time together. Tomorrow will be soon enough."

She sat down in front of the fireplace, and they talked and drank and fell asleep in one another's arms.

The Monday morning flight back to Myrtle Beach was one of Jack's best suggestions to avoid the weekend crowds. After they dropped off their bags, they drove to the Seafarers Mall. It was important to Beulah Jean to let Brandy and Dan know they were no longer persons of interest in either of the murder cases.

Brandy was behind the counter waiting on a customer. "Be with you in just a minute," she said when she saw Beulah Jean. Jack went to the back corner and looked at a bracelet with beautiful red sea glass on a shelf near the back of the store.

"So, any good news?" said Brandy as her customer left the store.

"I'm sorry it's taken so long to fill you in. The other day at the funeral I had an idea everything would be cleared, but without an arrest, I couldn't offer you anything positive.

"I take it I'm off the list," said Brandy.

"You are indeed. That piece of sea glass they found

in the man's hand was put there by his killer to throw off the authorities. He had other pieces in his possession. Somehow, he knew you would be questioned about your sea glass because he visited this mall on several occasions. In fact, he was the person taking over for Dan while he was away,"

"He knew Dan?" asked Brandy. "He's been very nervous for some reason. I think he knew one of the suspects. He's been in here several times asking if I heard anything."

"I'm on my way to see him. Maybe I can ease his mind. His case is a little more complicated, but I'm sure he'll be fine as soon as the killers are arraigned."

"Thanks for everything, Beulah Jean. You made my day."

Beulah Jean found Jack in the back of the store reading some brochure about sea glass. She let him know she was heading over to the Kitchen Cutlery and would meet him there when he was finished.

The store was busy. Dan had two people selling knives while he sat back and rang up the sales. She knew his health was still an issue.

"Hello, Dan," said Beulah Jean. "How are you feeling?"

"I'll feel a lot better when I'm finally finished with my angel whittler. I haven't been able to get in touch with him

I want him to get his merchandise out of my store. He won't return my calls.

"I don't think you have anything to worry about. He won't be returning any calls. He's been arrested."

"Oh my god. Is he the killer?"

"Looks like he will be arraigned soon. You should hear from Detectives Stone or Wexler within the week. Your name will be removed from the persons of interest list."

Beulah Jean could see his eyes tear up. This was harder on him than she thought. He made some quick decisions because of his illness. Then he made more decisions trying to cover up what he feared. Maybe he'll be able to heal completely with the knowledge that he is no longer a suspect.

He got up from his chair and gave Beulah Jean a big hug. "*You* are my angel," he said. "No more whittled ones."

Jack caught up with Beulah Jean as she was leaving Dan's store.

"Ready to go get the old lady?" he asked.

They picked up Miss Shelby at the Spa on their way home from the mall. Beulah Jean could tell she enjoyed her last few days being primped and pampered. They pulled into the parking space out back and unloaded their luggage, while Miss Shelby ran around the yard re-establishing her territory.

They heard the front doorbell ring before they came through the back door. It was Seth.

"Well. What a nice surprise," said Beulah Jean. "What brings you down to this neck of the woods?"

"I rented a cottage at the ocean for the month," said Seth. "I want to be in the courtroom when they bring in Max and Fitz."

"As long as you mind your manners," said Jack giving Seth a punch in the upper arm.

"I'm doing one better. I'm writing a book."

"Does it have anything to do with Bonnie and Scout?"

"It has everything to do with them," said Seth. "And the way in which they died."

"I got a text from Detective Collins last night," said Beulah Jean. "We haven't even discussed his findings."

"I've been working the story with the pathologist out

in Las Vegas," said Seth.

"Wait," said Jack. "How is he involved?"

Beulah Jean felt guilty not telling Jack about the pathologist's report.

"From what Collins said, the Myrtle Beach pathologist contacted the coroner out in Las Vegas who first discovered the method of killing with large plastic bags. He reexamined Bonnie and Scout's films and confirmed the blood spots were from the oils on their faces. They've changed their cause of death to homicide."

"So, there was actually a case on file to support Max's claims?" asked Jack. He wasn't just blowing off steam and making up stories when he told you guys at the brewery that night how his roommate in prison killed those women?"

"100% true story," said Seth. "I may not have been able to help Scout when he needed me, but I want to honor him by sharing this new homicide method with the world. Up until now Bonnie and Scout have been the silent victims. My first real novel will set the record straight and give them the medical notoriety they deserve. It will be named after the one the pathologist wrote in his report - *The Death Mask.*"

Carole O'Neill

Acknowledgments

After completing my first cozy mystery, *The Porch Sitters*, I realized I needed to write one more before going back to writing cold case mysteries. However, the transition from being a plotter to being a pantster took me to a place where I lost all control over what scene would come next, and how I would get there. After spinning in place for longer than I care to remember, my writing group and especially my husband, Jim, brought me through the dark and finally to the finish line. I can't thank you enough.

My faith in my muse was renewed when I saw a Forensic Files episode explaining how forensic scientist, Kevin Poorman, proved homicide in the Vicky Gillette case in Nevada. After repeatedly testing the plastic bag found in bed with her, he was able to prove her facial oils formed a perfect image of her face. He did, however, determine it would take more force than just resting her face on the bag. The pathologist would not have diagnosed a murder with the evidence the death mask left in her lungs without his research.

A special thank you to Pat Coloe, John Magliato and Cynthia Grey who allowed me to use their names in this mystery.

As always, the members of the Coastal Authors Network were more than supportive during the lengthy process of finding my muse.

My informative legal experts, always willing to offer the needed confirmation on my law enforcement questions will again remain anonymous as promised.

About the Author

Carole O'Neill is an award-winning producer-director with more than twenty-years-experience in broadcast television.

She spent her second career as a professor of media arts in Boston, and as a visiting professor at Coastal Carolina University in South Carolina.

In her retirement, she has enjoyed writing mysteries.

Carole O'Neill